SUDDEN MOVES

A Young Adult Mystery

Kelli Sue Landon

Outskirts Press, Inc.
Denver, Colorado

Sudden Moves
A Young Adult Mystery
All Rights Reserved.
Copyright © 2011 Kelli Sue Landon
v2.0

Cover Photo © 2011 JupiterImages Corporation. All rights reserved - used with permission.

Outskirts Press, Inc.
http://www.outskirtspress.com

Paperback ISBN: 978-1-4327-6713-6
Hardback ISBN: 978-1-4327-6714-3

Library of Congress Control Number: 2010943304

Outskirts Press and the "OP" logo are trademarks belonging to Outskirts Press, Inc.

PRINTED IN THE UNITED STATES OF AMERICA

To my husband, who makes me see the positive side in life.

Acknowledgements

A big thank you goes out to two special USPS retirees for reading my manuscript during my writing process. Without your emails and phone calls wanting more, this novel would have never been written! To my co-workers for your support and encouragement. Also, thank you to my family and friends for your inspiration. You were all a part of this story within my characters and have made my dream come true.

Chapter 1

The news came after Spring Break. Giles High resumed and Katie wasn't in attendance. One of the girls in my P.E. class said she was sick, but it wasn't confirmed by the faculty.

"Where's Katie?" I whispered to my best friend, Tami, who sat next to me in accounting class. "I'm dying to hear about her trip to Florida."

She shrugged, flipping through her accounting text book. "I dunno. Didn't you say someone said she was sick?"

"Okay class!" Ms. Runyon started with her lecture. "Hope you had a nice Spring Break lying on the beach, playing video games, or whatever kids do nowadays. Now it's time to get thinking again! Oh, and I know it's a pain to come back on a Friday, but it wasn't my choice to go on strike while you were off."

We all chuckled. We liked that Ms. Runyon was a big joker. She was around six feet tall, wore flannel and sprouted straight as a board gray hair which hung in her eyes. She wore no makeup or jewelry and appeared intimidating until she started talking. She was one of the most pleasant teachers I'd ever had in high school.

Instead of laughing at Ms. Runyon's teacher's strike joke, I contemplated on speaking up about Katie. I didn't ask Ms. Zimmerman in P.E. and I needed to know. I hated being the center of attention and often asked Tami to inquire about something since I was too embarrassed to speak up in class. The day was almost over so I decided to run with it.

"Ms. Runyon," I called, raising my hand. I felt my mouth go dry but I had to ask. "Where's Katie? I haven't seen her all day."

"Katie Brashers?" she asked as if there was another Katie running around.

"Yes."

"Yeah!" Brad Wilkes said from behind me.

"Oh," Ms. Runyon hesitated. "She moved to Orlando."

"Moved?" Brad said, his voice cracking. "She didn't even tell me."

"I'm sorry," Ms. Runyon said. " Now, let's get back to work. We have a lot of catching up to do."

People started talking to each other in muffled voices. I couldn't make out everything except Brad talking about how Katie never told him goodbye.

"People!" Ms. Runyon said loudly. "Enough!"

When class was over, people were still talking about Katie's move.

"I don't get it, " I told Tami as we walked together to

our lockers.

"Michelle, who cares?" she said. "It's Friday! You should be thinking of, like, going to Equalizer instead. Pick you up at 7:00?"

Equalizer was an under twenty-one dance club that was on the other side of Giles. Many kids from school hung out there and even some from the bigger city of Marian. That always seemed odd to me and Tami since Marian had everything including theaters and museums. Giles, on the other hand, had a small population of about four thousand and our biggest attractions were an ice cream shop and public swimming pool.

"Tami! You don't care why someone just disappears?" I asked.

"She didn't disappear. She was probably, like, planning on the move but didn't wanna tell anyone. She was weird like that. So secretive." She put her accounting book in her locker and took out a notebook. "One more class and we are outta here! Well, not really a class. It's screw off study hall."

"Yeah, well I'll see you later," I said, turning to walk toward my science class.

Just then Brad stopped me. "Hey, did Katie mention anything or drop any hints to you about leaving for good?"

"No," I said. I didn't know these two were serious. I mean, they went to the movies a few times but that was it. I always thought Brad was cute and hoped to go out with him someday. I envied Katie a little since she was the object of his affection. "I thought she would have returned the book I let her borrow a couple weeks ago."

He narrowed his eyes at me as if I were being petty.

It sounded awful to worry more about a book than Katie, but this book belonged to my grandmother and it had sentimental value. Elizabeth Benningfield wrote it about a love story set during The Great Depression. The story was fictional, centered around actual facts. It was out of print and my grandmother had it signed by Elizabeth in 1961. When I was a child she told me the cover was etched in gold. I thought it was real gold but my mother always told me it wasn't. That was a tale my grandmother liked to tell. My mother would kill me if she knew I loaned the book out.

"You'd think she would have told you she was moving, if you guys were close," I said, changing the subject.

"I was hoping we would get that way," Brad said. "It doesn't look like it now." He slowly walked off so I headed toward my science class.

I didn't know what else to say since time was running out and I had to get to class. Mr. Beaverton would tear me a new one if I was late. I'd seen it done to another class member and it wasn't pretty.

Chapter 2

"Don't worry about her!" said Tami on the school bus ride home.

I turned to her from the window. "I didn't even say anything!"

"Yeah but I can tell you are, like, spacing out or something. What is with you wanting to know why she left? Who cares?"

"I do!" I was flabbergasted at her attitude. "Mom will shoot me if she knew I loaned out that book!"

"Oh yeah, I forgot about that. Did she take it with her to Florida?"

"She said she wasn't going to. She wasn't done reading it yet and didn't wanna lose it," I explained.

"Well, then you can have someone go into the house and get it for you. You know, like a realtor or something."

We had to talk pretty loud to hear our voices over the excited freshman kids who were anxious to get home. They reminded me of animals who were locked up in the zoo and were now getting to run free in the jungle.

"Who says they are going on a vacation then not come home?" I was mortified. "That makes no sense. I wonder if anyone in Deedee's class has asked about her."

"Who?" Tami asked, fishing through her backpack.

I took a deep breath. "Deedee Thompson. Katie's sister."

"Oh, that little girl who is always hanging around her house? That's her sister?" She retrieved a small bag of cheese curls and ripped it open.

"Yeah, supposedly. They must be half sisters or whatever."

"Sounds like their mother has hot pants or something," Tami said with a chuckle.

"Tami!"

"What, you think they were, like, in an accident or something?"

Tami's suggestion crossed my mind just minutes before. She always seemed to take a lucky guess at what was in my head.

"I dunno," I said. "You never know what could have happened. I have heard about people getting killed on vacation."

"That's because of those mystery novels you read all the time."

"Yeah, especially since I'm in your mom's store more than you are!"

Tami's mother owned a book swapping store where you could take your old books in and exchange them for other books. She was also willing to sell them if the price was right. Tami never spent much time in the place since she wasn't a reader. She was more into movies.

"Look Michelle, it's probably nothing." She talked while chewing her cheese curls. "Katie could have lied about it being a vacation. I mean, nobody ever went to her house for dinner or sleepovers and she was new at the beginning of the school year. Nobody even knew where she came from."

"She told me she was from upstate."

"Whatever! Maybe her mom found a hot guy down there in Orlando and decided to stay."

That was a ridiculous reason, I thought, gawking at her.

"You never know!" The bus stopped. "Gotta go, I'll call you and talk you into going to Equalizer tonight."

"Yeah okay," I said.

I usually enjoyed going out to Equalizer, but I wasn't pumped up for it. Katie irritated me by leaving the way she did. We weren't close like best friends, but we had a lot of the same interests. She helped me study my accounting and got me through quite a few tests. This was the reason I loaned her my grandmother's book. She seemed to be level headed, so I thought she would take care of someone else's belongings.

I was hoping there would be some mistake and she was really home sick. She lived about five houses down from me and the thought occurred to take a stroll by her house. I was curious to see if anyone was still there.

When I got home from school, my mom was on the couch, reading the newspaper as usual. Our two year old basset hound, Buster, was lounging at her feet.

"Any good news in there?" I asked her.

"What?" She looked up over the top of the paper. Only her spiky bangs and eyes were visible. "Since when do you get into the news?"

"Have you heard about Katie?" I asked.

"White?"

"That's her mom's last name!" I said, irritated. "It's Brashers and why is that always the next question someone asks?" I plopped down into our leather recliner.

"Hey now, calm down! Anyway, didn't they go on some Spring Break trip to Florida?"

"Mom, they never came back!" I said "You didn't know?"

This was a shock. My mother was always reading the newspaper and hearing gossip from Cutting Edge, the salon where she worked. She would sometimes stop at Katie's house, but Luanne never let her in.

"No, Michelle, I'm not the neighborhood know it all! Maybe they are just not back yet."

"Ms. Runyon said they moved there."

"Moved?" She finally lowered the paper to look at me. "She never said a word about that."

"Who, Katie?"

"No, Luanne. I stopped over there to drop off that

sunscreen for their trip. The one I got you and you never opened. I hated to see it go to waste."

"Sorry, I'm never outside long enough to use it," I said. She was always bringing this up. I heard about all year how I was an introvert. What law stated that everyone had to be outside when it was nice weather? "So, what did she say? Anything about the trip?"

Her eyes wandered like she was trying to think. "No, just that they were packing and couldn't wait to go."

"Couldn't wait? Like excited? What about their house? Will it be up for sale?"

"Michelle, I don't know! I was only there for a minute! Luanne always talked to me through the door, you know that!" She got irritated when she had to explain anything to me. I was just inquiring, but this is how my mother was when I talked to her. "They rented that house anyway! Remember Mabel Watkins?"

I shrugged.

"She bought it a few years before she died."

I remembered some old woman living there before Katie, but never saw her. Mother looked at me as if I were stupid.

I had a feeling she was going to take a trip to the town market to fish around Luanne's co-workers. I was wondering if she quit her job or just left without saying anything. Mom wouldn't tell me anything even if she did know.

"Okay never mind," I said, rising to go to my room. Buster followed.

It didn't matter that Mom had just told me that Luanne never said anything to her about the move. Maybe that's because she was only there for a minute, dropping off sunscreen. Duh, Mother, is what I wanted to say.

She was always contradicting herself. I couldn't have a long conversation with my mother on any subject or it ended up in a heated argument where she was always right. It was a good thing Dad was a truck driver. Being away from home gave him a break from her. He was the lucky one.

Chapter 3

So, did your mom, like, find out anything?" Tami asked when she picked me up that night.

She was all decked out in a hot pink halter top with sparkly embellishments everywhere, even down to her blue jeans. Big silver hoops dangled from her ears. I went with my usual denim button down shirt, open with a striped tank underneath.

"What? Why would you ask that?" I asked.

"Michelle, we all know how Nancy is." She applied lipstick in the rearview mirror as she talked. "She hears, like, everything."

"Well, as far as I know, she hasn't found out. She's not home."

When we walked into Equalizer, the music was thumping and big multi colored lights bounced around to the rhythm of the music. It was packed as usual and the normal popular girls in the clique at our school were there, standing by the dance floor, sipping sodas through a straw.

"Can't they just gulp it down like a real woman?" Tami

said, bouncing her perfect curls with her hand.

"I'm gonna get one," I told her, before walking up to the bar.

"Get me one too, will ya?"

"Oh okay!" I laughed before motioning for the bartender.

Even though we were in a soda only bar, it felt like we were adults when we retreated to Equalizer. It was the place we could escape to. It cleared my head of stressing out about school work, home life with Mother, and Katie Brashers.

"I heard that they were planning this all along!" someone said, sitting on a bar stool next to me.

I got closer to hear over the music. They were yelling so it wasn't hard to make out what they were saying. I didn't know who the girl was since I didn't want to look at them. I just saw black hair and a black jacket out of my peripheral vision.

"You mean the trip?" another girl asked.

"It was a trip all right! Katie's mom was on some guy's trail."

"Why?"

"Well, it's like this. She was sleeping with this guy who was married and I don't know what happened, but suddenly this guy goes off to Orlando. Then Katie's family takes off to go down there. That's all I know."

Curiousity got to me. "Excuse me," I said. The girl turned and I recognized her from school. She was a goth with a long stringy black bangs almost covering her eyes, black eye liner and black lipstick. She wore neon green contact lenses that glowed. Her porcelain face made me think of a gothic doll. I was spooked for a second when she turned to glare at me. Her name was Krystal. How she knew Katie's family was beyond me. "Sorry I couldn't help overhearing. Do you know who the guy was?"

She just slowly shook her head and went back to her friend.

I'd seen both of them around school. Goth types usually kept to themselves so I was shocked to even see them at Equalizer. They would more likely hang out in a punk rock club or metal fest.

I returned to Tami and handed her her soda.

"It's about time."

"Yeah, well, I overheard the goths talking at the bar."

Tami laughed and almost spit her soda through her nose. "You were listening to them freaks and that's why I had to wait for my soda?"

"Well, you could have gotten it yourself!" I said.

"Hey hey hey now! Calm down, I was just joking. So what did Ms. Graveyard Freak have to say?"

"Her name is Krystal, but whatever. They were talking about Katie's mom."

Tami's eyes about popped out of her head. They resembled two big malted milk balls. "What about her?"

"Interested all of a sudden?" I asked sarcastically. "They said her mom is chasing some married guy."

"Holy crap! You gotta be kidding me! I never thought

of that and I think of everything!"

"It's gotta be a rumor."

"Why does it have to be a rumor? Women do that shit all the time."

"Tami it's gotta be! My mom would have heard about this."

"But, she wasn't home, when I picked you up. She may be, like, finding out all about it as we speak."

This was just way too intriguing for me to forget for the night. I wanted to stay for the gossip, instead of for the fun of being there. Unfortunately, we never heard any more stories except one in the bathroom about them being murdered by the mafia. I didn't know how that one got started, but Krystal's story sounded more real.

Mom was in bed when I got home so I turned in for the night. I laid awake in bed hearing the ringing in my ears from the loud music. Tami sent me a text on my cell, asking if I found out anything. When I replied that I had not, my phone rang.

"Tami!" I answered, whispering. "My mom could have heard that! You know I'm not supposed to get calls after 11:00!"

"I told you to put your phone in silent!" She sounded like my mother with that remark. "Sorry, I just had to call you. I heard from Brian who heard from his girlfriend that Katie's mom was into drugs. She went down to Miami to buy some and didn't have the money. Now she is missing."

Brian was Tami's brother. He dated some strange girls.

He hung out regularly at clubs and had a different girl every week.

"Tami, you believe something that came from Ms. Bimbo of the week?" I asked.

"Sorry Michelle, I know he sees some drugged out sluts, but I thought maybe this could be true. Miami is known for drug dealers and this girl would know."

"Whatever!" I was appalled that all these rumors were going around. Nobody knew Katie's family personally. It was almost as if everybody was making things up for drama. "They went to Orlando anyway. I gotta get to sleep. My ears are bugging me."

"Yeah, me too. Talk to ya tomorrow. Call me when you find out anything new!"

"Okay, 'night." I said before drifting off to sleep.

Chapter 4

The next morning, I was awakened by the smell of coconut. I came out to the kitchen to find Mother reading the paper at the kitchen table with her cup of German Chocolate coffee. This was her usual ritual on the weekends but with different coffee flavors.

I sat down opposite her at the table with my Sweet Sixteen magazine.

"I heard that phone go off at 11:30 last night!" she said.

I never could understand how she could be awakened by my phone when my door was closed and she sleeps down the hall. Unless she was lying there awake, listening. "Yeah, sorry. It was Tami." I thumbed through my magazine, not even paying attention to what was in it.

"Oh, you girls are so inseparable."

I changed the subject to get to something more important than a friend calling me on a Friday night. "So, have you heard anything?"

"About Luanne White?"

No, about Dad being a truck driver so he can get away from your mouth and leave me here to listen to you day in and day out, is what I wanted to say. She knew what I meant and it took a lot for me to bite my tongue.

"Yes, about Luanne or Katie or anything like that."

"Well," she put the newspaper down, "I did hear that she had a boyfriend and they all took a vacation to Florida. He even paid for the girls to go."

That was close to what Krystal was spouting off at Equalizer. "And?" I asked.

"That's it."

"That's it?" It was hard for me to believe that this was all she heard. "What about their house? Their furniture? The sudden move to Florida?" My one of a kind autographed book that Grandma left me? I thought.

She took a deep breath. "Michelle, all I know is that this guy was a secret she was keeping. Nobody at the market knew who he was. She was watching over her shoulder a lot. That's what her co-workers said, anyway."

Maybe that was because of the man's wife, I thought. I thought there had to be more to it than that. Maybe on Monday she will hear more at the salon.

I shrugged. "Well, okay, if that's all it is. I still don't get it." I started to get up from the table, but her next question stopped me.

"Why do you care?"

She stabbed my heart with that question. "Why do I care? Mom, Katie was a big help to me in Accounting. She actually had me thinking I could pursue it as a career! She said she wanted to be a teacher and liked helping people." I felt my eyes tear up but I fought the urge to cry. It hurt that my mother didn't allow me to feel anything. She could be hard as nails sometimes. I really liked Katie and was worried if something had happened. "How could I not care?"

"Accounting is too hard to pursue as a career," is all she said and went back to reading her newspaper.

I grabbed Buster's leash and decided to take him for a walk. I had to get out of the house, away from her. Anything for Mother to rain on my parade. If I gave any indication that I was thinking of doing something different, she found the negative side of it. Forget the positive. That wasn't Mother's style.

"Don't be snooping around their house, either!" she called as I attempted to put on Buster's leash at the front door. He wouldn't stay still. He kept jumping up and down as I tried to hang onto his collar.

"I won't!" I called back, almost falling over. I was losing patience. I had to go by that house. I didn't care what she said. "Buster! Be still so I can do this!"

He stopped his jumping and panting so I was able to snap the leash on.

"That dog loves his walks. I don't take him enough," she called again from the kitchen.

She was right about that. She never got out of the house unless it was to the store or work. She claimed it was bad for me being an introvert because I was young. Just because she was old, it was okay. Old people used their age as an excuse a lot of the time, I thought.

I hated that she sat inside all the time, in my business. Who was I talking to on my phone? What was I doing on the internet? Why did I suddenly have to use the car? The only time she didn't have a problem with me using the car was when I went grocery shopping for her. It was so much easier when Dad came home. He kept her occupied.

Chapter 5

It was a nice morning. All I needed was a light windbreaker. The air smelled clean, which put me in a better mood. It was as if my whole body got a sudden jolt and I was ready to take off.

Walking Buster was a difficult job sometimes. As we strolled down Redwood, past our neighbors, he wanted to stop and smell everything. No matter what it was, he had to find out why it was there.

"Buster, come on," I said, pulling the leash toward the road. "You don't have to check out every little piece of grass."

He panted as his little legs moved quickly to keep up.

Mother was still on my nerves and I always tried my best to get her off my mind, whether it was listening to music in my bedroom, talking to Tami, or walking Buster.

We were approaching Katie's house on the corner of Redwood and Oriental when Buster found a tree to hike his leg on. No cars were in the driveway. I was saddened to see a For Rent sign out front. I had an inkling that maybe they would be back and that this Florida move was a mistake. I waited for Buster to finish, then guided him to the front yard. It was the scent of freshly cut green grass in the air that reminded me Spring had arrived. It also meant that school was going to be out soon.

We walked up to the big picture window. I peeked inside, putting my hand up to shield the sunlight. All the furniture seemed to be in place. My heart sank as I noticed the absence of books. As a matter of fact, the walls were bare. Then again I had never been inside Katie's house before. Luanne could have been a strict housekeeper or the books could be in one of the bedrooms. When I stopped over, Katie always came outside.

I suddenly had an idea. The For Rent sign displayed a phone number. I just had to get up enough nerve to call it. If not, Tami would love to. I recited the number in my head over and over, and associated some of the numbers with birthdays, addresses or anything else that I knew personally. This was a trick I learned in grade school.

Buster whined, which was a sign he was annoyed at our stops, so I picked up the pace again. We exited the yard and turned down Oriental Drive so I could see the backyard. I thought maybe there would be something I'd see missing. Deedee had a swing set, so I was thinking that would be gone, but it was still there. Then I realized, how could someone take a swing set on a trip or move out of state?

"Hey there!" I heard someone call from across Oriental.

"Oh," I said, jumping from being startled. "Hi, Mr. uh." I couldn't think of the man's name since my brain was mush. I felt as if I had been caught doing something bad.

"Nichols," he said.

"Sorry, I forgot." I felt like an idiot as I guided Buster over to his yard.

"Yeah, I hated to see those girls go."

"You mean on vacation to Florida?" I acted stupid, really wanting him to get to the nitty gritty.

"I'm sure you heard," he said. "Oh what's her name," he patted his forehead with wrinkled fingers, "Uh, Luanne never warmed up to anyone around here."

"Yeah, I know." I already knew this, come on and tell me what happened, I thought. "My mom visited sometimes."

"Oh yeah, I did see some people stop over there every now and then, but not for long." He came over and pat Buster on his head. "I had me a hound once. I love these dogs. Lookin' to get another one sometime, but don't know how long I'm gonna make it."

I just stood there, waiting for more. He wasn't going to stop with that was he? I thought. How could he just change the subject?

"Um. Mr, Nichols?"

"Yeah, hon?" He was still petting Buster.

"I was just wondering, do you know why they left and never came back?"

"Well," he stood back up to face me. "I just saw them leave with suitcases that day, um, let me think." He patted his forehead again.

My heart was pounding. I hated the feeling of anticipation.

"I do remember a car picking them up."

My heart skipped a beat but I was trying not to show my excitement. "You do? What kind was it? Did you see who was driving?" The questions came out of nowhere. This old man would definitely tell I was prying and that's not how I wanted to sound.

"No, lemme think." He took his hand away from his forehead. "There was a dark blue SUV. I don't know what kind it was. I never saw the driver."

"SUV?" I asked, puzzled. For some reason, I kept thinking that if she had a guy, he would be driving a sports car. But then how would all the suitcases fit into a sports car?

"Yeah, that's what it was," he said as if he were still thinking.

"So the guy never got out?" I asked.

"Guy? What guy?"

"I'm sorry Mr. Nichols," I said with a nervous laugh. "I just assumed a guy picked her up."

"Oh, well, that car has been there on and off for a while."

"Oh, I see." I was trying to sound casual.

"Luanne was awful good lookin'," he said, gazing over at the house. "Boy, she would be out in that yard in those little blue jean cutoffs. Ya know, with the fringe?"

"Okay, I'm going to get Buster back now." I pulled

my windbreaker closed since it wasn't zipped up. I did not want to hear anything about this old man's desires. It creeped me out. What if he was looking at me like that? "Bet she got herself a boyfriend and took off, outta this town. People were talkin' about her, ya know?"

"Yeah, I will see you later Mr. Nichols." I waved, turning to leave.

"You take care now!" he waved back.

I started walking home and looked back at Mr. Nichols a few times. The whole time he was watching me.

"Old man Nichols?" Tami asked me on the phone.

"Yeah! He was creeping me out!" I couldn't wait to call Tami after getting Buster home. I had my phone with me during the walk but felt the need to get as far from Mr. Nichols as possible.

"Michelle! That man has got to be ninety or something."

"So what? You should have seen the gleam in his eyes when he was talking about Luanne. I also think I asked too many questions at once. I don't have the patience and I had to know what all he saw."

"The guy probably thought he was, like, being interrogated or something. You made the poor old man nervous," she said. "Where are you? Is your mom home?"

"Yes, unfortunately! I'm downstairs."

I was resting on an old musty smelling couch in the

basement. It had a wood frame with hard cushions. Buster sometimes lounged on it when it was too hot for him upstairs. Our basement wasn't well taken care of, but it was the only place for us to do laundry.

"I was wondering why you were talking so low. Ask her to let you come over."

"She won't let me use the car," I said. "I hate asking her for it."

"Hey I know, I'll pick you up and say we are, like, going to the mall."

"Are we going to the mall?" I asked. I was terrible at lying so I wanted to tell Mom the truth.

"I dunno," she said.

"I don't feel like it. It's too crowded on Saturdays with screaming kids everywhere."

"Okay, let's have lunch somewhere. Just say that."

"All right, a ham and cheese wrap sounds good right about now."

Chapter 6

So much for screaming kids!" I told Tami as we sat in a booth at Wrap n' Roll.

There was a couple with two little boys who kept slapping each other a few tables away. There was a baby bawling it's head off across the aisle from us.

"You wanna move?" she asked.

"No, this is fine. I would think they could take those kids outta here since it looks like they are done eating." I purposely rose my voice and added, "This isn't a playground!"

"Calm down, Michelle."

"Sorry," I said, taking a deep breath. "I'm just on edge."

"Why, because old man Nichols was, like, looking at you? Checking out your young figure?"

"He wasn't looking at me!" I hollered. That made the kids stop fighting and stare at me.

"Jeez!" Tami said, biting a french fry. "What has got you all riled up?"

"That old pervert, that's what."

Tami chuckled, unwrapping the paper from her sandwich.

I took a small bite of my wrap. This place had the best sandwiches around. I got sick of the usual fast food restaurants and loved coming here.

"You wish you would have stayed there and, like, found out more from the old man?"

"Oh," I swallowed. "I almost forgot, I have a phone number!"

"Phone number for who?" Her eyes bulged out of her head. "Katie?"

"No, the landlord of the house."

"Yeah, so?" she said, taking a monster bite of her jalapeno and pepper jack sandwich.

"I was thinking that if you wanted to, we could call and ask about the house."

"What's that gonna do?" She spoke with a mouthful as her face turned beet red. The heat of peppers never bothered Tami. I was convinced that her mouth was immune to any hot pepper known to man.

"I dunno," I said. Why can't she just agree with me or come up with something to ask? Tami was good at that. "Maybe ask about who lived there before. Like did they take care of the place? Is the house furnished?"

"Okay, I guess. I don't see how that's gonna, like, solve this mystery of where they are now." She had a sarcastic tone. "Why did Luanne take her kids to Florida? Why did an SUV pick them up? Better yet, why did she decide to move to a much sunnier state than Illinois?"

"All right, Tami that's enough!" I said a little too loudly.

The fighting boys were on their way out with their parents. They looked back at me before exiting. "I think it would be odd if they left their own furniture. Like they were planning on coming home, but never did."

"So, you think they are, like, murdered or something?" She took her napkin and wiped sweat from her forehead.

I just sat there. I didn't know how to answer that.

"Come on Michelle," she said. "Tell me you don't think that."

"I don't know what to think," I said. "Something is just weird about this."

"You just wanna find your book."

"That too," I admitted. "But that's not the only reason."

"Okay I'll tell ya what," she took another fry, started at the top and bit it down repeatedly as it disappeared into her mouth. "I will make the call for you. You are going to, like, end up asking too many things."

Yes! I knew she would want to do this. I recited the number as she picked her phone up off the table and punched it in.

"It's ringing," she said.

"Watch how much you say the word like," I cautioned her. "It sounds too much like a teenager."

She waved her hand away like she knew what she was doing.

I was on pins and needles, wondering if someone was going to answer.

"Yes, I am calling about the house for rent on Redwood Drive." Tami was doing her best to sound like her mother.

"Yes, 3805, that's it. Oh, well how much is it a month?"

I sat there, my eyes fixated on Tami, waiting as I leaned toward the table. I thought I was going to be able to hear the other side of the conversation, but no such luck.

"Oh, that's a little higher than I thought it would be."

I snickered.

Tami motioned for me to be quiet, putting a finger to her lips.

"Is it in good shape?" she asked. "I mean, did the people who lived there before take good care of it?" A pause. "Uh huh." Another pause. "Is it furnished with appliances, sofa, bed, such essentials as those?"

I had to keep from laughing. This was too much, hearing Tami talk like some professional.

"Uh huh, I see. Well, could I come by and look at it?"

I shot back from the table as my mouth dropped. I had no idea that was going to come out of her mouth.

"Okay, that'll do. I can be there in two hours. I got stuck working today so I may be a little late. Sure thing. See you then. Take care now." She flipped the phone shut, smiling to herself.

"What the hell are you thinking?" I hollered.

"Hey, calm down!" She said firmly, her eyes narrowing. "You wanted me to do this!"

"This isn't gonna work!" My adrenaline was running rapid. "This person is not gonna believe you are an adult looking to rent a place!"

"Yes he will. I just gotta go home, get all gussied up and be there in, like, two hours." She continued eating her sandwich like nothing had happened.

"Tami!" I hollered again."

"Michelle!" she mimicked me. "What is your problem?"

I started breathing heavily. "We are so gonna get busted."

"Over what?" She laughed through a mouthful of food. "We are just looking at a house for crying out loud. I think you should stay in the car."

"Oh, no way! I am so going in that house! If it weren't for me, you wouldn't even be going!"

"Michelle, cool it." She looked around the restaurant. "You are making people stare."

My eyes gazed around the place. I lowered my voice, reaching for my soda. "So, was it furnished already?"

"Yeah, he said everything in the house belonged to his mother who passed away a year ago. She lived there."

I tried to slow down my breathing. Must be Mabel Watkins, I thought.

"Are you gonna make it?" Tami was still feeding her face.

I couldn't eat any more. "Sorry, but I just don't wanna blow anything and have my mom find out."

"Why are you so afraid of her?"

"I'm not afraid! I just get sick of all her crap, that's all. I'm sick of her telling me what's right and what's wrong."

"That's a mother for ya." She sucked some soda through her straw.

"She specifically said not to go to that house and I did."

Tami shrugged. "That's a teenage girl for ya."

We laughed and discussed how Tami planned to be fixed up to meet the landlord.

Chapter 7

"How about this?" Tami asked while taking a black dress out of her closet. "I wanna look nice. The guy had a hot voice."

"Black for spring?" I asked, ignoring her remark about his voice.

"It's sleeveless and made of rayon! Besides, do you think this landlord is a fashion expert?" she asked sarcastically.

Just then my phone rang. Ugh! It was my mother.

"Hello?" I said answering it, as if I didn't know who it was.

"Michelle, where are you? You should have been home by now."

"Oh, we stopped at Tami's house. She had a CD I wanted to borrow." It was easier for me to lie over the phone.

"Okay, just checking. I didn't think you would be eating this whole time. I'm going to run to the market."

"Okay." I said before hanging up.

"What was that about?" Tami asked, holding the dress up to herself and looking in the mirror.

"Mom. I have no idea why she called. Wow, she is going to the store. She calls it a market like we are in 1955 or something. She's probably gonna snoop around again about Luanne."

"Hey!" Tami's brother Brian opened her door and popped his head in. His hair was colored jet black and spiked straight up. He wore a ring through his bottom lip and one in his eyebrow.

"What do you want? Get outta here!" Tami yelled.

"Did Arabella call while I was out?"

"Who is that? NO!" She slammed the door in his face.

"Wow! He just comes in like that?" I asked her.

"Mom told him not to be doing that." She continued to look at herself in the mirror. She lowered the dress and frowned. "We are going to have to park on another street and walk. We don't want your mom to, like, see my dad's car there."

"Oh yeah!" I felt a panic come on again. "Oh Tami, why did you have to worry me?"

"Calm down, will you? I'm wearing this. I have earrings and a bracelet to match. I have time to curl my hair, don't I?"

"I guess," I said, checking the time. "Pin it up like you did that one night we went out."

"Oh when I let the curls dangle?"

"Yeah, you looked more sophisticated."

"Yeah I did, didn't I?" she said, smiling her perfect

pearly whites. "And I get to, like, pile on the make up!" She jumped up and clapped like a little kid in a candy store.

When Tami got done, she looked like a million bucks. Her olive skin had always been immaculate. The black dress had a high neckline with rhinestones across the collar and was formed to show off her curvy figure. She even put on panty hose and wore high strappy sandals with a wedge heel. She claimed that was her spring fashion touch since I commented on the black being all wrong. Her hair was pinned up as strands of brown curls fell to her shoulders.

"Let's go!" She grabbed her purse. "Like my little clutch?"

I didn't realize she was going to take a different purse. "You look like you are ready for a night out."

"Maybe I am! See how I bounce?" She moved her head from side to side.

"I hope you are talking about your hair."

She let out her loud laugh that I found annoying at times. I almost had to plug my ears.

"Well, what am I gonna do?" I asked.

"Just act like you are my sister and I had to, like, pick you up on the way. No big deal. We can just say you are moving in with me and wanted to see the house or something."

"Okay," I said reluctantly.

I was a tad jealous she was the one who got to dress up and play adult. I looked like I had just got out of bed, compared to her. My hair was hanging in my eyes and I had no make up on. I was so paled faced, but I was in a hurry to get out of the house when we decided to go eat. My hair had a tendency to frizz and never curled easy like Tami's did. On the other hand, she did the dirty work by calling about the house, so I should have been happy.

Tami seemed to be acting like this was all fun and games and I was the one worrying. I didn't know what would happen to us if we got caught. Maybe just my mother grounding me and never letting me out of the house until I turned eighteen. That was bad enough, but better than the police nailing us for fraud. We were pretending to be other people, unless Tami decided to use her real name. Then it technically wasn't fraud, at least I thought.

"Where are you going?" Tami's father asked us on our way out of her house.

"Job hunting," she answered without stopping.

I just followed, not even looking at him.

"Like that?" He said louder as we walked out. I wasn't sure if he said anything else after that because I couldn't hear him when the door shut. I thought for certain he was going to run after us, but I was wrong.

Chapter 8

Job hunting?" I asked as we pulled out of her driveway. She just waved her hand as if to say, don't worry about it.

When we arrived, we parked down the street on Oriental, giving us a glimpse of the driveway. I looked over at Mr. Nichols's house, but he wasn't outside. That was a relief. He could have been looking out the window, but I couldn't tell. I knew the old man didn't have much of a life. He was usually sitting out on his porch in his old metal rocker.

"So now what? The landlord isn't here yet," I said. "Are you going to use your real name?"

"Yeah, why not? It's not like he knows who I am."

I shrugged. "Well, I just had to know what my phony last name was, that's all."

She laughed. "Michelle Simmons. That's cool, don't ya think?" She flipped down her visor and looked in the mirror to check her hair. "Just let me do the talking."

All of a sudden she was in charge of this operation. It was me who wanted to find out more about Katie and where my book was. Tami never seemed to care about anything until it got juicy or dangerous. She was the type who got bored easily even when it came to going to the movies all the time, the same restaurant, or even liking a particular guy.

Just then there was a car pulling into the driveway. My heart skipped a beat. It was a dark blue SUV.

My mouth went dry. "Oh boy."

"What?" She looked over at me. "Why is your face all red?"

"Oh nothing, just that now it's for real." I didn't want to tell Tami I noticed the SUV, linking it to Mr. Nichols's story. She would accuse me of being paranoid again, plus I didn't want her getting nervous all of a sudden and crack under pressure.

My hands were shaking as we walked up to the house. I tried to hide it from Tami by putting my hands into the pockets of my jacket.

I glanced at the SUV as we walked by. Nothing unusual inside that I could see. It appeared spotless inside and out.

Tami knocked on the door while I glanced back at the license plate. It wasn't a vanity plate which made it hard to memorize. I tried my best at it but then the screen door opened.

"Hey there!" a man greeted us, letting us in the house. "How are you doing?"

"Oh, just fine," said Tami with a fake smile. "We passed the house accidentally. I didn't care to turn around."

"That's fine," he said, looking around the living room.

"Well, as you can see, I kept everything here that belonged to my mother."

"Hmmm, I see that. That's good because I don't intend on keeping much of my old furniture. And my appliances?" She put her hand up. "Pffffffft!"

I was trying hard to keep from laughing. Tami was waving her hands around femininely, trying to act like such a sophisticated adult. I covered my mouth with my hand as if I were deep in thought and looked around.

The house smelled so clean and fragrant, almost as if a country scented air freshener had just been sprayed. Everything was in pristine condition with no trace of dust or grime. The walls were a light blue color with a white ceiling. Everything appeared spotless down to the light tan carpet. Doorways were arched which I always admired in houses I had been in. There was a ceiling fan that held three bulbs. The fixtures reminded me of frosted drinking glasses. The lamp shades were nostalgic and frilly, as if they belonged in the nineteen twenties.

"Nice coffee table," I said, trying to throw in my two cents somewhere.

"Oh, this is my little sister!" Tami moved near me and grabbed my shoulders. "She is planning on staying with me until college."

"Oh, that's nice," the guy said. "I'm Sean, by the way."

"Yeah, I remember you telling me that on the phone. I'm Tami." This sounded like a flirty tone to me. If there's anything I can spot, it's Tami's voice when she really likes a guy.

"I know." He let out a fake laugh, probably to make her feel good about herself. This guy was prim and proper, wearing a navy blue polo shirt and wire framed glasses. He wasn't the type Tami went for. She preferred jocks, the kind of guys who were muscular and fearless. Sean reminded me of a scrawny computer nerd.

Tami followed Sean into the dining room area and kitchen. I could still hear his voice loud and clear. "The woman who lived here left some things behind, which can be very annoying," he said.

Tami let out a fake laugh. "I know what you mean."

I mocked her laugh quietly to myself as I continued eyeing the living room. The couch and matching loveseat displayed a blue floral pattern. No books were in sight. I had a feeling Katie took the book with her to Florida. I was worried that she may have tried to sell it. I regretted ever letting her borrow it and vowed to never trust anyone with my belongings again.

I noticed the oak end tables had doors as well as the coffee table. I looked inside the end tables, but there was just a phonebook inside one of them. It looked pretty tattered, so I took it out and thumbed through it. I didn't expect to find anything, but inside the front cover was a phone number sloppily written. There wasn't a name, but I put the number to memory. I could hear Sean's voice getting closer to the doorway so I put it back and closed the door.

"You like those tables?" He asked.

"Oh yeah," I said while reciting the number in my head.

"Nice doors for storage."

"Would you like to go upstairs and see the bedrooms?"

"Sure!" I said excitingly, playing the game. "Can't wait to see where I'm gonna sleep, Sis!"

Tami gave me a smirk.

There were two bedrooms upstairs. The master bedroom had beautiful hardwood floors blanketed with a giant round maroon rug. The bed had a brass headboard and looked straight out of a magazine advertisement. The second bedroom had bare hardwood floors and two single beds.

One for each girl, I thought. This was perfect. Almost too perfect. How were they able to find a nice place with three beds exactly?

"I have a question," I said, finally speaking up about something. Tami shot a quick look at me.

"Yes?" Sean asked.

"Why did your mother have two twin beds?"

"They were in our family. Did you know my mother? If you are from the area, you may have met her."

I shook my head. Oh no, I thought, he is going to catch on to us.

"We're not from here," Tami said.

"She lived here for about five years. She bought the house, then left it to me when she died."

I nodded, hoping to get off of this subject.

Tami looked out the window and commented, "Oh, nice swing set."

"You have kids?" Sean asked negatively.

Oh, no, I thought. Please, Tami, don't say yes.

"Oh no," she said. "It's just an observation."

"The yard was nice at one point," he explained. "The woman who was here didn't take care of it so there's patches where I had to throw down grass seed."

On our way out I walked into the kitchen. There was a super shiny hunter green tile floor that matched the counter tops. Sunlight seeped through the window blinds and shown beautifully on the china plates that hung on the walls. I noticed a knife missing from a butcher block on the counter.

"Your set is missing a piece," I pointed out.

"Oh yeah," he said without blinking an eye. "It got lost and I never had time to replace it."

I wondered if Luanne lost it somehow or he used it for something and got rid of it. My mind wandered back to the SUV. Was he the one who took them to the airport? Things seemed fishy. A missing knife and this smooth talking computer geek started to eat away at me.

We didn't talk much more before leaving the house. I looked again at the license plate on the SUV when we left. I didn't know what I could find out. I was sure the DMV wouldn't give out information about someone's vehicle so I tried remembering it just in case I would see the car again around the neighborhood.

I had written down the phone number when I returned from the house. I never told Tami anything about it. I didn't want her setting up a meeting with this person, whoever it was. I thought repeatedly about calling it just to see who answered. If the number showed up on the phone bill, I could tell Mom I dialed the wrong number by mistake. Whether she believed me was another story.

I spent Saturday night watching movies and Sunday studying. I tried my best to focus on school work instead of Katie's house.

Sunday night Mother didn't talk much during dinner.

"How's school going?" she asked.

I stopped and stared at her, holding my fork in mid air. She never asked about school.

"It's okay," I answered, eating the horrible goulash she made. I about gagged every time I put it in my mouth. She may as well not even stir up the tomato paste, because that's what it tasted like. Pasty. I had to wash every bite down with my cranberry juice.

"Hmmmm," she said, chewing. "No news on Katie or her mom?"

"No," I answered, probably a little too quickly. I didn't want to discuss it with her. I was happy she didn't say anything else about it.

After dinner, I went to my room and fished the phone number out of my purse. I thought I could ask for a fake name just to see if this was a business or a person. I didn't think I would accomplish anything, but it was worth a try.

I just took a deep breath and thinking like Tami, said out loud, "I'm not afraid of this. What's gonna happen over the phone? They're not standing in front of me." Then I thought it could be a long distance call with another area code anyway, so the call may not work. Thinking that way helped give me the courage to do it.

I punched in star sixty-seven to block my number from showing up on a caller ID, then the phone number.

A woman picked up after the second ring. "Hello?" she said in a pleasant voice.

"Tami?" I asked purposely.

"No, this is Betty."

"Oh, I'm sorry, I must have dialed the wrong number."

"That's okay dear."

"Okay, thanks," was all I could think of saying.

This could be someone who Sean's mother knew, I thought. There's probably not even a connection to Katie.

I wrote down the woman's name by the phone number anyway.

Chapter 9

The next day in the cafeteria, Tami asked if I had heard anything else.

"I told you this morning on the bus, I didn't! How would I hear anything else since then?" I asked.

"Maybe gossip around school?" she said, loudly over the chatter of other students. "What's the matter with you?"

"Nothing." I shrugged, taking a bite of cheesy pepperoni on a paper thin pizza crust.

We sat at our usual round table against the wall. The tables at Giles High seated four people at the most, instead of the normal picnic style tables most schools had. I loved that we could talk more privately this way.

"I was thinking maybe we can go back and look at the house," she suggested, opening her milk carton.

"Again?" I asked, chewing. I didn't understand why she wanted to look at it again. Nothing else could be found as far as I was concerned and I didn't want to get busted.

"Michelle, people look at houses more than once if they really, like, want a specific one."

"Well, what are you going to say to Sean? He is gonna think you really want the place. Before long you are gonna be paying your first month's rent!"

She started picking at her pizza. "You don't have to go with me."

I stopped chewing, holding my pizza slice. The pepperoni was about to slide off as the crust sloped down toward my plate.

"What?" she asked. "Don't look at me like that!"

I shook my head. "You are unbelievable." I put my pizza slice down, not even wanting the rest of it.

"Why? How else do you think we are going to, like, get to the bottom of Katie's disappearance?"

"Why are you interested in this all of a sudden? A few days ago you didn't care where Katie was."

She paused as if she were thinking, sipping milk from her straw. "Okay, the truth is, I would like to ask Sean out."

This was typical. "Tami, he is way too old for you!"

"How do you know?"

"He is a landlord for crying out loud!" I didn't realize how loud I spoke until Tiffany and her clique glanced our way. I also noticed Brad Wilkes turning his head toward us in my peripheral vision. Krystal even looked up in her zombie like stare.

"Quiet around Queen Tiff," Tami whispered, her eyes wandering the room. "He just took over that house when his mom had it. That doesn't mean he's, like, too old." She looked around the room before continuing. "And he is twenty-seven if you must know. I asked him when we were in the kitchen, looking around."

This was actually a surprise since I thought Sean looked more like early twenties. "He is really up there. And you are underage," I reminded her.

"Not for long. What, another year and a half? "Doesn't matter."

"It was just a thought anyway," she said, shrugging it off.

I couldn't tell if she was telling the truth or just wanting to get off of the subject. I wasn't about to tell her about the phone number I found.

I glanced over at Brad who quickly looked away. I wondered if he was listening. I wanted to tell him I found that number and that we were in Katie's old house. I had to find a way to talk to him without Tami around. If not, I could call him if his phone number was listed. Nowadays not many people had a landline, but his parents were pretty old so I didn't see them even having a cell phone, let alone depending on one.

I started making plans in my mind about what to do.

"Michelle?" Tami asked.

I snapped back to reality, looking at her. "Yes?"

"What's the deal?"

"What do you mean?" She could always see through me.

"You were eyeing up Brad."

"No I wasn't!" I felt my face heat up. I was sure it was turning red.

"Sure!" she said with an attitude.

I drank my milk and self consciously worried if Brad was watching.

As luck would have it, I happened to see him before accounting class when I was at my locker.

He approached me. "I'm sorry if I was eavesdropping at lunch," he said nicely.

"That's okay." I had no time to waste. This was my chance. I was nervous, but I had to ask him. "Brad, I wanna talk to you outside of school about Katie. Can I call you?"

"Sure!" He looked really happy which surprised me. He opened his notebook and wrote down his cell number.

People started to stare when he tore it off and gave it to me. I knew this was going to get back to Tami so I had to think of a reason Brad would write something down and hand it over. Then I thought, so what if he gave me his number? Maybe he was just being concerned for all they knew.

"Thanks," I said. My heart was racing so I took a deep breath. "Oh and can you not say anything about this in class? I don't want anyone to, you know, think we are getting involved, you know, with Katie's disappearance or anything else. Not that there's anything else, but you know." I was rambling so I just shut up and walked away.

I was embarrassed in Accounting with Brad sitting behind me. What did he think about my rambling? Did he think I wanted to go out with him since I asked for his number?

I was happy for once that Ms. Runyon lectured through the whole hour. That kept Tami quiet and my mind off Brad. I was not, however, looking forward to the bus ride home.

"Okay, spill it!" Tami said, sitting down next to me on the bus.

The news had gotten around already.

"Spill what?" I said, trying to sound innocent.

"Michelle! You know what!" I couldn't tell if she was going to laugh or be angry.

"No, I don't know what!" I said, mocking her.

"Brad, that's what! I heard he, like, gave you his number."

I was prepared for this. "Wow, big news about someone giving me a piece of paper with a phone number on it," I said sarcastically.

"Well, you don't have to be a smart ass about it!" She tore open a small bag of potato chips. "So, what's up?"

"Oh, he just asked if I had heard anything more about Katie. I said no, so he gave me his number in case I found out."

"Found out what?" She held the bag open toward me.

"Anything, I guess," I said, taking a chip. Crumbs fell everywhere when I crunched into the salty goodness.

"Michelle, you aren't going to, like, tell him we were in the house and acted like renters, are you?" Her eyebrows sunk down the middle of her forehead.

"Stop looking at me like that! Of course not!"

"Okay," she said with a smile. "I didn't think you would."

The rest of the ride home was pretty peaceful. She kept going on about whether or not she should call Sean.

I tuned out most of her talking, thinking about what to say to Brad if I called him. I really wanted to, but was afraid Tami would find out what was discussed between us. I was sure she was afraid Brad would go telling everyone we were in Katie's house, then it would be around the whole school, eventually getting back to our parents. I just had to rehearse what I was going to say to Brad when I called him.

Chapter 10

Mother was watching her Monday night television show which kept her occupied while I could quietly call Brad from my room. I didn't want to sit in the musty basement. She would think I was talking to Tami anyway. I hated the thought of her knowing I was talking to a boy. She would want to know everything about him and I wasn't about to tell her, especially since he was Katie's boyfriend.

I decided to text him first to see if it was okay to talk. I could have texted him more, but we didn't have unlimited texting and I didn't want to rack up the bill and never hear the end of it. If Mom saw the number on the bill, I would say it's a friend from school and leave it at that.

He answered on the first ring.

"Brad?" My heart was racing again. I couldn't calm down so I started pacing the floor.

"Yeah, Michelle? I've been waiting for you to call!" He sounded excited. "What did you find out? Anything? Do you know where she is?"

"Hold on," I said. He was throwing too many questions at me. "I found out from one of her neighbors that a dark blue SUV picked them up that morning."

"Yeah?" he said.

I didn't know how to tell him the next part. "That and I was able to look inside the house, but all I found was a phone number written inside a phone book. I called it and someone named Betty answered."

"Who's that?"

"I don't know. I just said I had the wrong number and hung up."

"Well, okay. I would have talked to her."

I was hoping he wasn't upset. He seemed agitated.

"I still have the number if you wanna try." I really wanted him to call since I already had.

"I wanna find out more first. Could you get me in that house?"

I stopped pacing. "No, but I have the number to the landlord. He has a dark blue SUV."

"WHAT?" He was so loud, I had to hold the phone away from my ear.

"Brad, calm down. That doesn't mean anything."

"What kind of SUV? There are a lot of them out there, but he may be the one."

"The one to what? He may have just taken them to the airport."

"What about her mom's car? Where was that when all this was going on? Still in the driveway?"

I hadn't thought about that. I remembered she did have

a car in the driveway. It was a small brown car with a hatch back.

"Brad, that didn't even dawn on me. I don't think it was there. I didn't ask the neighbor. I guess I assumed she drove it to Florida."

"Did the neighbor say she got into the SUV? Was it just Katie and her sister?"

"I dunno." I felt like an idiot. "Brad I'm so sorry."

"Don't worry about that now, could we talk to that neighbor again? I am gonna call this landlord but I would like you to take me to the neighbor if you can."

That creeped me out but then if Mr. Nichols sees that I have a guy with me, maybe he wouldn't get all dirty mind-ed again. I often replayed his words about Luanne in my head.

"Okay, I can walk my dog after school tomorrow. Can you meet me up at the house?" I asked.

"Sure thing. Oh, and thanks." he said in a pleasant voice. "I know it's hard to think of everything at one time. Don't worry about forgetting the car."

"Well, it was still stupid of me, that's for sure. Oh and I noticed that a knife was missing from a set on the counter."

"Oh, that's probably nothing. My mom is always losing stuff when she cooks."

"I guess," I said, not knowing what else to say. I still wasn't sure what to make of it and I didn't want to alarm him if it was nothing.

"I will talk to you tomorrow. This just amazes me. I

knew there was more to this than her just up and leaving."

I was thrilled I was going to see him tomorrow. I just didn't want to seem stupid like I did, forgetting about Luanne's car. At least he was happy that I gave him the information. I felt better about telling him instead of Tami. Who knows what she would have done with this Betty person. I would have to tell him to keep this whole thing quiet so it wouldn't get around school. I didn't even think of that during the phone call. I sent him a text about it real quick before going to bed.

Chapter 11

School went pretty good the next day. Tami kept going on about Sean and how she planned on calling him.

"Tami, be careful," I told her during lunch. This time it was chili dogs. "You are gonna blow our cover."

"What? He knows my real name. Besides, it'll just be for coffee."

"Since when do you drink coffee?" I could not get over her behavior. Tami's parents drank coffee like water and she always complained about the smell of it.

"Oh, it's okay. I don't mind it with, like, tons of sugar and milk."

I chuckled. "This guy has you changing yourself already." I took a bite of my half cold chili dog.

"So? Who doesn't change themselves for someone?"

I shook my head as I swallowed. "You hardly know this guy!"

"But I will get to know him! That's the whole point!"

"The whole point of what?" I suspected she was checking him out undercover.

"Of meeting a nice guy to have fun with!"

"Fun?" Or was it sex she was talking about?

"Oh, never mind. I think he's hot."

That was basically our conversation. This guy being hot for reasons I wasn't aware of.

After school, I changed into my lime green clingy top and added some dangling earrings. I wanted to look different for Brad since he always saw me in my same old school clothes. I pulled my hair back into a ponytail since I couldn't get it to do anything that morning. It puffed out like a big pom pom connected to the back of my head, but it was going to have to do. The texture was getting to be like straw.

I was going to have to weasel some time from Mom for an appointment at Cutting Edge. When she put color in my hair, it made it so much more manageable. She would only let me get it colored the exact same way or a little darker or lighter. She didn't believe in young girls coloring their hair since no gray was present. I only got to do this every six months, so I was due.

I was hoping Mom would have still been at work when I got home, but no luck. She never said anything when I walked in the house. She hadn't talked to me that much over the weekend which was odd, but I enjoyed it. There were times when she was down over Dad being gone and not calling.

I snapped the leash on Buster's collar and left. It was a nice sunny day. I didn't even need a jacket.

I met Brad up at the corner, by Mr. Nichol's house. I

had to say, he was looking fine in a green sleeveless shirt and blue jeans. I always knew he had a great build from the tee shirts he wore in class. I noticed his little red car in Katie's driveway which gave me a jolt of panic.

"Did you call the landlord?" I asked, wondering if that was his reason for parking there.

He shook his head. "Not yet. Which neighbor?" he asked as I approached. I was hoping for at least a hello or a smile. His blue eyes sparkled in the sun. I instantly felt weak looking into them.

Katie, you were so lucky, I thought. How could you leave this? I put the thought of Brad's appearance out of my mind, as hard as it was.

"He's not outside," I told him. "Why did you park there?" I could not believe I asked him this. It just came out.

"What's the big deal about that? I've parked in her driveway before."

I shrugged.

"What house is it?"

I pointed to Mr. Nichols's house and he started heading up the driveway.

"What are you doing?" I asked, my heart rate speeding up.

"I like this guy!" said Brad, smiling. "He would always talk to us when we were hanging around Katie's yard. I rarely got to go inside her house."

"Rarely?" I asked. "So that means you have been inside her house?"

"Just a couple times. Come on," he said, heading up to Mr. Nichols front door. "This guy don't bite."

We walked up onto the old wooden front porch. The boards creaked so loud, I was sure Mr. Nichols was going to know we were there and wouldn't have to wait for a knock. Buster was busy sniffing at the wood as he walked.

Brad knocked a few seconds later.

Mr. Nichols appeared at the screen door. "Yes?" he said, putting on his glasses. "Oh, hey how are you?" he asked Brad before looking at me. "Hello again, little lady!" He opened the door and came out onto the porch. He seemed so happy to have visitors. A big grin spread across his face, showing big brown teeth. "You wanna come in for something to drink?"

"Oh, no thanks, Mr. Nichols," Brad said.

He pat Buster on the head and sat down in his old metal rocker. He took out a pack of cigarettes from the pocket in his robe. He had pajamas on under it, at least it appeared to be pajamas, and a pair of brown slippers.

"Sit on down there." He pointed to some plastic crates that were turned upside down.

"No thanks." I said. I was too nervous to sit.

Buster plopped down on the wood and rolled onto his side for a nap.

Brad sat down before talking. "I was going to ask you something about the blue SUV you saw picking up Katie."

He gets right to the point, I thought.

Mr. Nichols lit a cigarette and looked at us while blow-ing out smoke. "What?" he asked, as if he didn't know what Brad was talking about. "You mean old Mabel?"

Oh no, I thought. He is losing his memory and now I look like an idiot. What's Brad going to think of me now?

"Oh, yeah, the young family other there. Lemme see, the car that picked them up." he said, remembering. At least I hoped he was remembering what he told me.

"Yes, that's correct," said Brad. He was acting professional which I really liked. This was much more real than Tami's performance. "Do you remember seeing Luanne's car there too?"

"Oh." He scratched his forehead. "Um, I don't think it was there. Well, where was it?"

We just waited as the look on his face told me he couldn't remember. He was staring into space as he rocked.

"Who got into the SUV?" Brad asked.

"Um, I just saw the girls get in with their suitcases."

"The two sisters? Katie and Deedee?"

"Yep, that was it," he said, taking a drag of his cigarette.

Brad and I just looked at each other.

"You didn't notice anything else going on over there?" I finally spoke up. I didn't want Brad to think he had to do all the talking.

"Nope," he said. "Nuttin out of the ordinary. I just thought they were goin' on a trip. I'm always watchin' my game shows durin' the day so I don't pay attenion all the time. Oh wait. Now I do remember seeing some blonde woman over there a few times."

"Blonde woman?" Brad asked. "Luanne, you mean?"

"No no. Luanne was good lookin'."

Oh no, here we go, I thought.

"This was an old woman. Not as old as I am, but I wouldn't take her to bed."

Brad laughed. I did too, because I didn't expect Mr. Nichols to utter those words.

"Did she have a grandmother?" I asked Brad.

"Not that I know of," he said, wiping his eyes from the laughter.

"Did she have long blonde hair or short?" I asked Mr.Nichols. "Maybe pinned up?"

"All I know is the style reminded me of that goofy Broadway actress. What was her name? You remember that old broad? Carol somethin'?"

Brad laughed again. I was relieved he felt comfortable with this old man.

"Who?" I asked.

"Oh, never mind," he said with a wave of his hand. "You youngsters."

Brad was back to wiping his eyes. "Do you rememeber what she drove?"

"Um, no," he said, with his head down like he was trying to think. "A bug maybe."

"A little car?" Brad asked.

He nodded. "Yep."

"Okay well, we won't keep you," Brad said, rising from the crate.

"Keep me from what? Smokin' myself to death?"

"Thanks for your help," Brad told him.

I tugged on Buster's leash to wake him up.

"Oh, anytime. Come back again! I love havin' people over."

As we walked away, Brad kept chuckling. "He is a riot," he said quietly.

"Yeah, that's Old Man Nichols, as Tami calls him."

When we got to his car, he asked for Betty's number.

"You remembered it?" he asked after I told him.

"Yeah, it's not that hard. I have a way with remembering things. I associate them with dates, birthdays, stuff like that. You know like number ten means October. Number 26 is the date of my birthday."

"Wow, I'm impressed!" He said.

"Well, what about this blonde woman?" I asked, hoping he could shine some light on the subject of this mysterious woman.

"Are you thinking what I'm thinking?" he asked, leaning against his car, folding his arms.

I hoped he didn't know what I was thinking at that point, because I would have hopped into his car right then if he asked me to leave with him and never return. I'd even take Buster.

"What's that?" I asked, waiting to see what he was thinking.

"This woman may be Betty."

"Oh." I snapped back to reality. "Yeah, that's what I was

thinking too." Of course that wasn't true.

"I'm going to call and talk to her," he said.

"Now?"

"No, probably later. I will have to figure out how to find out who she is. I also gotta call that landlord."

"Do you need help?" I don't know why I asked that. It came out sounding stupid. Why would Brad need help talking to someone? He was great with Mr. Nichols.

"No thanks," he said. "I can manage it."

My heart sank. I was hoping just maybe he would invite me over and we could call Betty and Sean. I wouldn't have been able to go with him, but it would have been nice for an invitation anyway.

"Well, will you let me know tomorrow if you call tonight?" I asked.

"I'll call you if I find out anything."

I smiled. It excited me to even think that Brad would call me. I hoped I wasn't blushing. "Okay, well I'm going to get Buster back home."

"Okay, I think I'm gonna talk to some of the other neighbors."

"Now?" I asked. "You going door to door?"

"Is there any other way?" He laughed.

"No, I guess not." I wanted to go with him, but I really had to get home before Mom got suspicious.

"Okay, see ya," I said.

"Thanks for the info."

I nodded as my mouth went dry. I took a deep breath

and hoped I wouldn't fall on my face from being weak in my knees. Tami would love to hear about this, but I wasn't about to tell her. It was tough keeping this a secret, but I had to try no matter how bad it burned inside me.

Chapter 12

As I was turning in for the night, getting cozy in my bed after a hot bath, Tami called. I was hoping it was Brad. It was because of him that I kept my phone in vibrate that night, instead of silent mode.

"Hello," I answered in almost a whisper.

"Hey! You in bed already?"

"Tami, it's ten o'clock. What's up?"

"You keeping quiet, huh?"

"Yeah, what is it?" I asked again. I didn't like sneaking calls for fear of getting my phone taken away. I should have just let it go to voice mail, but I was curious as to what she wanted.

"Well, I did it!" She sounded ecstatic.

"Did what?" I bolted upright in bed. Did she find out what happened to Katie? Did she get into the house again?

"I asked Sean out!"

I slowly laid back down, disappointed. "Oh, that's it?"

"Michelle! You know how much I, like, wanted to go

out with him! And he said yes!" She sounded ecstatic, giggling like a twelve-year-old.

Tami's parents didn't care if she was on the phone late at night as long as she was out of their hair. I wished I had parents like she had.

"I told you this was a bad idea."

"Oh, he doesn't know how old I am."

"What are you gonna say if he asks?"

"Eighteen of course! That's the age I always use when I lie."

"You haven't done this before!" I said, a little too loud.

"So? That's the age I've always, like, wanted to use!"

Just then my door swung open. I hit the off button and hid the phone under the covers. "What is it?" I asked, trying to sound groggy.

"Are you on that phone?" Mother asked harshly.

"I was," I said. "It was just Tami. I told her I was in bed."

"That phone is supposed to be silenced!" She flicked the light switch on. "How many times do I have to tell you that?"

I shielded my eyes with my hand. I was not expecting the light to come on. When my eyes focused somewhat, I could make out a glass in her hand. She was drinking. She drank more since she quit smoking.

"What is wrong?" I asked.

"Don't act concerned with me!" She said louder. "You are just like your dad! You don't care about me!"

Her remarks told me Dad hadn't called. This happened once in a blue moon and it angered me. Thanks Dad! I thought. This was all I needed while hiding my investigation from Mom.

"Get to sleep!" she said. "Or no more phone!"

"I will," I promised. "Sorry, Mom."

She slowly closed the door and walked away. Tami never called back so I sent her a text real quick telling her I'd talk to her tomorrow. Mother worried me more than Tami did as I laid awake, wondering why I had so much going on at once. When it rained, it poured. I worried about Mother drinking and hoped Dad wasn't in an accident or running around with some other woman. I didn't want my parents going through a divorce, no matter how unhappy Mom was. I just wanted Dad to come home. I did my best to go to sleep, but it took a good hour before I got there.

Chapter 13

Sorry I hung up on you," I told Tami on the way to school.

"Yeah, no shit!" she said. "What happened with Mama Nancy?"

"Drinking again. I wonder if she will make it to work." When Mother was hung over, her mood was worse which was bad for customers.

"Well, I had the best thing to tell you last night and I didn't, like, get my story out!"

"Oh, sorry Tami but I had a family crisis!" I said with an attitude. "It's not all about you, ya know."

She took a deep breath and looked ahead at the frazzled seat in front of us. "I know. I'm sorry about your mom."

I shrugged. "It is what it is. Dad not calling."

"Hope he does soon."

"Me too. Now what happened with Sean?"

"We are going to dinner!" Her eyes lit up. "Tomorrow night at Desiree's!"

"A school night?"

She nodded, making her curls bounce. "He thinks I, like, go to college so I'm not lying."

"Whatever," I said.

Desiree's was an upscale restaurant complete with mood lighting, romantic ambiance and a piano player for everyone to enjoy while they dined. She was on cloud nine. I don't recall ever seeing Tami this happy. I worried, however, what the consequences were going to be when Sean found out who she really was.

"Tami, this can't turn out good," I told her. "I have a bad feeling about the guy."

"I have it under control. It's just a date for crying out loud!"

"Just keep your guard up. I think he is hiding something." I knew it was going to turn out to be more than a date. Tami never went on just one date with a guy.

"I gotta talk to you," Brad told me just before lunch time, while I was at my locker.

"What?" I asked, my heart rate speeding up. I actually found this thrilling, talking to him in the hall with everyone present. "Did you call the landlord?"

"Yes, I did. I'm going to look at that house. That guy sounded like a scum bag on the phone."

"What do you mean?" I couldn't stop looking at his perfectly formed arms, peeking out under his short sleeved tee shirt.

"Just with the way he was talking. It was like I was taking up his time or something."

"Have you talked to Betty?"

"Had to leave a message on her voice mail. I did give her my number because I have to see who she is."

I wondered briefly how dangerous that was going to be. "What time are you going to see the house?" I was also worried that Sean would get suspicious of high schoolers looking at the house.

"Supposed to meet him around five."

There was a pause between us. I so wanted him to take me in his arms right there, but deep down I knew it wouldn't happen. Shut it out of your mind, Michelle, I told myself.

"Are you going to tell him who you are?" I asked, coming back to reality.

"No," he said, looking around. "I'm going to say I'm a senior but looking for a place for my elderly mother. My parents are older than normal anyway so it doesn't feel like a lie."

I chuckled. I found it ironic that Tami and Brad both knew how to dance around lying. "Will you call me after you get done? I just wanna know how it went, if that's okay."

"Oh, I will," he said before walking away.

I scanned the hallway and found that people were looking my way before walking to class. Rumors were going around, I was sure. I could just imagine what they were all thinking.

"Well?" Tami said from behind me.

"Well what?" I turned in surprise. "Are you sneaking up on me?" I asked, shutting my locker.

"No! Why so offensive?" she asked. "Going to lunch now or what?"

"Yeah, whatever."

She was getting on my nerves. Tami had been my best friend since kindergarten, but I was sure I was going to hear all about her date with Sean during lunch.

"I have to figure out what to wear on my date," she said, opening her carton of milk at the table.

"You have a whole closet full of crap," I said, unwrapping my cheeseburger. It had a burnt smell.

"Yeah, but this is Desiree's! I have always dreamt of going there!" She stared off into space, her dark brown eyes sparkling. "I always wanted someone to take me there. I hear their Crème Brulee is to die for."

"Do you even know what that is?"

"No, but it's gotta be good, doesn't it?"

"You were gonna go to this place with someone you were in love with, weren't you?" I asked her as I assembled my cheeseburger the way I wanted. Always with pickles on top of the onion.

"Well, I was but I couldn't, like, pass up this invitation."

"Didn't you ask him out?"

"Well," she said stumbling over her words, "yeah I did, so?"

I held my cheeseburger in mid air before taking a bite.

"Did you pick the restaurant?"

She started sipping her milk through the straw, ignoring my question.

"Tami?" I said. "Did you pick the restaurant?"

"Yeah, so what?"

"You plan on getting serious with this over-the-hill guy?" I sunk my teeth into the driest, flattest burger ever made. Not to mention it was tough to chew.

She waved off my question with her hand. "I can't wait forever for Mr. Right to come along."

I made a face from the taste of my burger as I chewed. "Well, you asked him so that means he is gonna want you to pay."

"WHAT?" she gasped.

I looked around. "Shhhhh! People are looking."

"That's not gonna happen," she said quietly. "I will make sure it doesn't before we go."

Tami always had a way with words and I almost wished I could hear the conversation she was going to have with Sean about paying for dinner.

"He has property anyway, so he can afford it."

"Property?" I asked. "How do you know?"

"Well," she was stumbling again, "he's a landlord, so he's gotta have property."

Then it hit me what Tami saw in Sean. She thought he had money. Still, something was off. I sensed she was keeping something from me with the way she was talking. She rarely stumbled over her words.

"Tami, what did he say about his job?"

"Nothing, just that he, like, owned different houses and condos all over."

"That was it?"

She looked me square in the eyes. "Yes! We didn't have that long of a conversation before I asked him out."

I believed her. I felt that there was more that Sean was going to tell her. About what, I wasn't sure. Maybe the house or his job. Was he married? I didn't see a ring when we met him, but that didn't matter. If he was, I couldn't see him taking a date into a public place. Maybe he was okay, but I was skeptical. I took a deep breath as I thought about the situation. There was a lot going on at one time and I wasn't sure how to deal with it.

For the rest of our lunch period, I listened to Tami ramble and ramble. I wasn't even sure when the last time she studied.

I knew my grades were slipping in science class when Mr. Beaverton commented on my late homework. I had forgotten we had an assignment due. I hated science. It took more concentration than what I was able to give at that point, but I had to buckle down.

I hoped to stay in my room and get some homework done that afternoon. Besides science, I had an accounting balance sheet due at the end of the week and a composition paper due at the beginning of the following week. It was a good thing I worked ahead in my independent study history class. I was a rare breed when it came to taking a class on my own. I actually worked faster since I didn't have to sit and listen to a teacher lecture, which took up more work time. My fun classes such as typing and home economics were a breeze so I didn't have to study outside of the classroom. I was not up for a boring night, but my work had to get done and it wasn't going to do itself as much as I wished it would. I hated homework, especially with everything else that was going on.

Chapter 14

I grabbed a soda and a small bag of corn chips before I got started on my homework after school. I was happy Mom wasn't home. She hated me having lunch type food at home. I hoped to take Buster for a walk sometime around five. By then I'd be ready to get out of the house since Mom will be home.

Everything was going well, then I heard Mom's car pull up around four-thirty.

The shop must have been slow. I waited impatiently in my room until five o'clock.

"Everything okay?" Mom asked as I came out. She was making coffee.

Surprised at her question, I answered, "Yeah, just doing my homework."

"I thought maybe you were sleeping or not feeling well since I didn't hear any loud music coming from your room."

"No, I have a lot of homework. I'm gonna take Buster for a walk."

"Hey, I got you some hot fudge sundae toaster pastries at the store."

She was actually in a good mood. I wondered why, but I wasn't about to ask.

"Thanks." I grabbed Buster's leash. This miraculously awakened him from sleep.

"They were on sale," she said. "You look tired."

"Lot of homework," I told her again.

"Yeah, that's what you said. Hey, you wanna go out to eat tomorrow tonight?"

This was strange. I liked it, but curiosity engulfed me. "Sure." I hardly ever got a night out with Mom, just the two of us.

"The Pizzeria okay?"

Something was definitely not right. That was my favorite place to go for the best deep dish pizza piled high. Mom wasn't crazy about it, so this made me a little on edge.

"What's going on?" I asked.

"What?" she stopped pouring water into the coffee maker and gawked at me. "I thought you loved The Pizzeria."

"I do, but you don't."

"Michelle, it's been a while since we've had some quality time outside of this house, don't ya think?"

I nodded. I could hear Buster panting uncontrollably, with a few whines to tell me to hurry up.

"Okay, let's go Sweetie," I told him, snapping on his leash.

Brad had to be at the house by now, I thought. I would

just walk by and not worry about what was going on. That's what I told myself, so I tried my best to stick to it.

The breeze was warm and welcoming as I walked up the street toward Katie's old house. It helped calm my nerves, but I still wondered if Sean and Brad would be outside. Buster was walking fast so it felt like he was walking me.

I passed by the rental house to find Sean's and Brad's vehicles in the driveway. I wondered what was going on inside. I looked up ahead as I walked and saw Mr. Nichols waving at me from his porch.

"Hey there!" he called waving. "Come on over!"

I thought maybe he had something to tell me so I took him up on his invitation.

"Hey there, Mr. Nichols," I said, breathing hard, the porch creaking under my feet.

He got up from his rocker. He was wearing his robe again. "Does the pooch there want a hot dog or sumthin?"

"Oh, no thanks. He's fine."

"I have some in the fridge and they go bad since we have to get a package of eight," he said, going inside.

He emerged a short time later, tossing a hot dog down to Buster and popping open a beer for himself.

Buster wolfed it down like he was starving.

"You wanna weiner?" he asked, sitting in his rocker.

"Um, no," I said. Boy, Tami would be laughing at that comment, I thought.

"So what's goin' on over there?" He nodded toward Katie's old house.

"I dunno," I answered, looking over that way.

I took out my phone and punched in a text to Brad that I was at Mr. Nichols's house.

"You kids and that textin'. Is that what they call it now? Textin'?"

"Yes," I knew what was coming next. I got so tired of hearing adults have a conniption fit over people texting. "It's not just teenagers who do it and I'm not driving for crying out loud," I told him without looking up from my phone.

"Back in my day, we didn't have phones. We went to each other's homes to talk to each other."

"Well, it's different now." I snapped the phone shut and hoped Brad would see my message so he would come over and rescue me. Mr. Nichols had nothing important to say. He was just a lonely old man who wanted company. I actually started feeling sorry for him.

"Someone must be lookin' at that place. I seen that red car before though," he said.

"What else didn't you have back in your day?" I asked to get his mind off Brad's car. What if he sees Brad come out of the house? What then?

"Oh, uh," he looked instantly at me, "well, televisions for one thing. But I like that invention."

"We all like inventions," I told him. "What other inventions do you like?" I could not believe how fake this sounded coming out of my mouth.

"Well, electricity is a good one. Oh and the fridge. Ya

gotta have that one. But, my favorite is the push up bra. A genius had to think up that one."

Oh no, I thought. I stepped into it again.

He was going on and on about the push up bra. Available in different colors and all. I tried my best to ignore him as I periodically looked over at the house. I wished I could have looked in the windows or that they would have come outside to talk. I didn't think I could hear them, but I could read their body language.

Just then, Brad ran out of the house. Sean came barreling after him. I wanted to holler for Brad to get his attention, but Sean would hear me and look over. Then our cover would be blown.

"Well, lookee over there!" Mr. Nichols said, pointing.

Brad bolted to his car, slammed the door, threw it in reverse and squealed the tires, heading down the road, away from Mr. Nichol's house. Sean stood at the driveway, his hand on his hips, watching Brad disappear.

I felt a stab of disappointment. I wanted Brad to read my text, telling him I was just across the street. I wanted him to see me and tell me what happened. Furthermore, I wanted him to scoop me up into his car and take off somewhere, away from this place.

"I know my eye sight is goin', but wasn't that the young man who was here before? I can't remember his name. Bud, was it?"

"Well Mr. Nichols, I should be going," I told him, giving Buster's leash a short yank.

"You sure?" he asked.

"Yeah, I have homework to do." I said anything to get out of there.

"Okay, then. Stop by anytime."

We headed off the porch and toward my house. As I passed the rental house, I saw Brad's car come toward me. Sean's car was still in the driveway, but he went inside. Oh no, I thought. What if Sean sees me talking to Brad? What if Mr. Nichols sees us? How long is it going to take for news to get around that we are checking out this house? On the other hand, I was relieved that he came back. He got my message. He wanted to see me.

He stopped catty corner from the rental house and I walked to him. He never got out of the car or turned off the engine as I stood outside his window.

"Thanks for messaging me," he said with a smile. He was breathing hard and his face was flushed. "Get in. I gotta talk to you before the scum bag sees me."

I nodded. "Is it okay for Buster to climb in the back?"

"Sure, that's fine."

I was thrilled. Brad didn't mind dogs riding in his car which told me he was a dog lover. I walked around to the passenger's side and got in.

"I'll drive down a few blocks and pull over," he said.

I looked ahead and saw Mr. Nichols standing on his porch, looking back at us. I was worried. I wasn't sure if he would talk to anyone about this, but I hoped my mom wouldn't find out. I had never dated anyone and I was sure she would not approve of me getting into some guy's car whom she hadn't met.

We pulled over at the corner of Oriental and Cedar which was the street than ran behind the rental house. We couldn't see Mr. Nichols from where we were.

"What's going on?" I asked as he shut off the engine.

He took a deep breath and looked over to me. "He's married."

"What?" My heart pounded against my chest like a drum. I suspected this, but I wanted to know how Brad found out. "Did you ask him?"

"Yeah." He chuckled.

"What's so funny?" I noticed that I came off offensive. "I mean, why is it funny he is married?" What about Tami? I thought. I had to tell her, but what if this wasn't true?

"He thought I was coming on to him. That's why he chased me out of the house."

I had a hard time believing this. It wasn't that I thought Brad was lying, I just found it strange that someone would take a question like that so serious.

"Maybe he just told you that he was married since he suspected you liked him."

"No, I asked him that plus some other stuff. I wanted to know if he had a girlfriend first and he said no, then I asked if he had a family. He said he had a wife. Then I went on about Luanne. I asked if he had any involvement with the woman who lived there. That's when he went nuts."

"What do you mean, nuts?"

"He got all red and shit. Wanted to know why I was asking such personal questions. I told him it was all around town that she was having an affair with a married man."

"And?" I asked. "How is that a come on?"

"He accused me of being queer and came after me. He stumbled on the coffee table when he ran after me. It's a good thing I was parked behind him."

"Yeah, well did you look around? Did you see anything out of the ordinary?"

"Michelle, I was only in that house a few short times. From what I saw, everything looked normal."

"Did any other neighbors see anything going on?" I asked, referring to him going door to door.

"No. Luanne seemed to keep to herself from what it sounds like. She didn't associate much with anyone."

"Did you happen to see any books?"

"Nope," he said.

I put my hands to my face and elbows to my knees. Buster was whining.

"What's wrong?" he asked, laying a hand on my shoulder. My heart skipped a beat. He was touching me!

"Nothing," I said, wiping my hands across my oily forehead. "I just don't see why Katie didn't contact anyone after going away. How am I gonna get that book back?" I felt myself panicking. I didn't want Brad to see this side of me.

"Don't worry," he said, his voice tender. "I don't intend to give up. Especially after going this far. I really miss

Katie. This is why I'm trying so hard."

I felt a tinge of jealousy. "I miss her too." It wasn't a lie. I did miss her, but maybe not as much as he did. "I'm sorry about all of this."

"It's not your fault," he said. "I want you to tell me anything you find out. Speaking of that, I'm calling that Betty woman again. She never called me back."

"You wanna do it now?" I was curious to know who she was.

He gave me a surprised look. "I guess I can." He hesitated when he took his phone from his drink holder.

"What?" I asked, noticing his behavior.

"I have a hard time talking when people are listening to me, that's all."

I knew that feeling but there was no way I was getting out of the car. For a second, I wondered if what Brad was telling me was right.

Buster whined like he was giving me a warning. Was he telling me to get out of the car?

"I gotta get Buster home," I said, putting my hand on the door handle.

"Well, wait a minute."

I looked into his blue eyes. How they made me weak once again. I had heard most serial killers are good looking and smooth to get the ladies interested.

Stop it, I thought. I had known Brad since sixth grade when he moved to the neighborhood. I never knew him personally, but there was never anything bad going around about him or his family. His parents were retired. His dad had been a carpenter and his mom, a doctor's secretary. They had a nice house close to where most of the jocks and cheerleaders lived. Brad wasn't all that popular since his parents kept him on a short leash. He wasn't allowed to have parties like the popular kids had.

"What is it?" I asked.

"I'm going to call her. Hopefully she will answer this time."

I nodded, letting go of the door handle.

Buster whined. "Buster, shhhhh!" I told him. He abruptly plopped down onto the seat.

Brad searched through his phone for his dialed calls and hit the button to redial Betty's phone number.

"Hi, is this Betty?" he asked. "My name is Brad Wilkes."

My mouth dropped. I was glad she answered the phone, but I had no idea he was going to tell her his name.

His eyes were on me the whole time. "I found your phone number written inside a book at Luanne Brashers house. She used to live there. Yeah ma'am, Brashers."

I shook my head and mouthed the word White for Luanne's last name.

"I mean White," he said, shrugging at me. "Okay, I'll hold." He shook his head at me. "I forgot that was her mom's last name. I am screwing up big time."

"No, you're not, but should you have told her your real name? I mean, who is she?"

"I dunno, but I figured the truth can't hurt. The truth sets you free right?"

I shrugged. I wasn't sure if that was entirely true. If I told my mother the truth about me sitting in a guy's car and making phonecalls about Luanne and Katie, I wouldn't be set free. I'd be banished to my room for the rest of my life.

He put his attention back to the phone, "Yes? I am Katie's friend from school. I hadn't heard from her since her vacation and I just wanted to talk to her." A brief pause. His mouth dropped. "Okay, listen lady I don't know who you are but-"

What? I mouthed to him. I wanted to know what was going on. He came closer and put the phone out so I could hear. I felt his breath on the side of my face and got a whiff of his cologne. I did my best to stay focused.

"We are not allowed to give out information to where our children are," Betty said. "This is a legal matter. These foster children are protected."

"WHAT????" I yelled without thinking.

Brad snapped the phone shut. "What did you just do?" He was mad, glaring at me.

"Foster children?"

"Michelle, I cannot believe you did that!" He raised his voice. "I was close to finding out something."

"No, you weren't!" I yelled back. "She wouldn't tell you anything! What did she say before, when you called her lady?"

He looked at me for a short time without saying anything. I wasn't sure if he was going to tell me or throw me out of the car.

"She said I was not allowed to know anything about Katie or Luanne." He put his head down. "She is a representative for Guardian Angels."

"What's that?"

"Some adoption place. Child services I guess."

I blew it. "I'm so sorry, Brad. I wasn't thinking."

"I really miss her, Michelle." He looked over at me as his voice softened. "I lay in bed at night and wonder where she is."

I wasn't up to hearing about him missing her. I wished he talked about me like that. "Maybe they really did go to Florida. If she is a foster kid, someone else could have adopted her down there. Or maybe Luanne found a nice house down there and adopted her."

"Boy, you live in a candy land world, don't you?"

I took offense to his remark.

"Okay fine!" I said angrily. "Come on Buster."

"Wait!" he said.

I ignored him, letting Buster out of the back seat. "Sorry if I'm trying to be positive here, okay? I gotta get home."

I walked off, looking back a few times. Brad's car didn't move.

Chapter 15

I couldn't believe it. Katie wasn't Luanne's daughter. That explained the different last names. Deedee must have been fostered too. If they were adopted, their last names would have been White like Luanne's.

I couldn't stop thinking about it that night, which made me lose sleep. That resulted in my being grouchy on Thursday. The day was basically a blur with Tami talking about her date. That actually kept her from asking me questions about whether or not I had heard anything else. I didn't utter a word about what Brad and I had found out. He didn't say anything to me that day. I guess we were both a little upset and felt awkward about talking to each other. I knew I did. Maybe I shouldn't have stormed off, but he upset me with the way he was going on about Katie, and then talking down to me for being positive.

"You've been quiet today," Tami said on our way home from school.

"I didn't get much sleep last night, like I told you earlier."

"Well, you have been worrying too much. Just chill out and take it easy," she said before bringing up her date again.

I laid down after school and napped for a couple of hours. I felt better that night when me and Mom went out to dinner, but my mind was still wandering so I wasn't enjoying myself like I had hoped I would.

"What's wrong with you?" Mother asked as we waited for our pizza while sitting in a booth. She had her hands folded on top of the checkered table cloth. Her nails were painted a shiny coral color.

The aroma of melted cheese and pepperoni surrounded us while Italian music played overhead. The Pizzeria made me feel like I was actually in Italy. How I wished I could drink wine. That would certainly make me feel better.

"Oh, nothing," I said. "I was just wondering, if I was adopted or fostered by you, would you keep it a secret?"

"Michelle, what is with that head of yours?" Her face scrunched with the look of confusion. "Where did this come from? You think you were adopted?"

"No!" I said with a laugh. "It's some assignment we have to do."

"For what class?"

I cracked. I wish I had Tami's mind so I could come up with the right explanation at the right time. "I dunno."

"Michelle, what is going on? Why would you ask that?"

I took a deep breath, as I saw the waitress coming with our beverages. I remembered Brad saying the truth would set you free but I didn't entirely believe it. I took a chance anyway. "I heard something about Katie and Deedee not being Luanne's daughters," I said after the waitress left.

Her eyes almost bulged out of her head. "Is that what's going around now? First it was her having an affair, then the mafia came into it, now the kids aren't hers?"

"Well, they were fostered I guess."

"Oh, these rumors," she said, shaking her head and taking a sip of wine.

"Is it true?"

"Well, how would I know?"

By working in a salon, I thought. "You won't tell me, will you?" I said, squinting suspiciously.

"Now, stop it!" she said a little too loudly. "Do we have to fight on our night out?"

I paused, looking down at my lap. "I'm sorry. I didn't mean to get upset." I really wanted a good night out with her. They were very rare.

I noticed my phone started to vibrate so I checked it. Tami was calling. This wasn't the time to listen to her brag about Sean, the married scum bag. I didn't want to answer and interrupt dinner with Mom so I ignored it. She was supposed to be on her date anyway.

The thought of Sean made me want to ask Mom a question, so I went ahead with it. "Mom, you know the old woman who lived in Katie's house before?"

"Yeah," she said. "Mabel Watkins."

"Did she have a son?"

"She did, but I guess he never claimed her. I heard they

had a falling out years ago. Supposedly he was her only living relative so he got that house. Why?"

"No reason. I just heard he was showing the house and I don't remember who lived there before Luanne moved in."

"That's because she stayed inside all the time. She even had groceries delivered to the house. Very lonely person. Her health was bad also. You will get like that if you don't start spending more time outside."

I got tired of her bringing that up, especially when she didn't get out all that much. "I walk Buster," I pointed out. The poor dog would never walk if it was up to her.

"Yeah, but that's only for a few minutes a day. Why are you asking about that house, anyway?"

Oh no, I thought. What do I say now? I sucked some of my soda through my straw, thinking.

"I was just wondering, that's all. I wasn't sure if Luanne lived there before she took in Katie and her sister." Good save, I thought. Maybe I was getting better at this lying, but I changed the subject. I had to know what was going on with my father. "So, did Dad call?"

"Well, yes he did!" she said, her face lighting up. "He's been so tired lately. He is coming home tomorrow night or Saturday."

"You didn't tell me." I was a little ticked off at this.

"I just found out today. I wanted to make it a surprise."

I nodded. "I see." I knew there was a reason she was in a good mood. Mother was always happy when things went her way.

"Aren't you happy?" she asked.

"Oh, yeah I am. I just have homework on my mind." I lied which was normal when I talked to my mom. I was happy my father was coming home, but I couldn't get Katie's situation out of my mind, not to mention my book. I also wondered how long Brad sat in his car after I left. At least Dad could take Mom's attention away from me while he was home, unless rumors started flying about me and Brad hovering around the rental house.

"How long is he going to be here?" I asked as the pizza arrived.

"Maybe for the whole week. I'm so glad to have him back!" she said with a wide smile, showing her nicotine stained teeth.

"Me too!" I said excitedly, looking at the deep dish of cheesy cuisine in front of me.

Taking my first bite of pepperoni heaven, Tami crossed my mind. Why would she be calling? Maybe she found out he was married. I made a point to call her back when we got home.

Our conversation shifted to my hair. Mom agreed to do a color on me over the weekend which I was happy about. She paid for the supplies out of her own pocket since I didn't get allowance. I was having a happy stress free dinner with my mother at my favorite restaurant. It was the little things in life, such as this, that made me happy.

Chapter 16

On the way home, I got a text from Tami. She said that Sean broke their date. My mind started racing. Was it because of what happened with Brad? I couldn't wait for Mom to get us home so I could call her in private.

"Maybe tomorrow at the end of my appointments I can get you in. Blonde highlights work good for you, right?" Mom asked, driving.

I nodded. "Yeah, they always do the trick."

"What's wrong?"

"Nothing," I said. "Just thinking about Dad coming home." I had to stop this transparent way about me or she was going to find out about my investigation and the book I was missing.

"Maybe we could go to the movies Saturday night."

I looked over at her, amazed. I could not remember the last time we all went out as a family. It thrilled me to see us getting closer. I just hoped Dad was up for it.

"You could bring Tami if she wants to go."

Was I dreaming? Hopefully Tami will be happy to go.

From the phone call and text message, it seemed like she was in panic mode.

We got home and I thanked mom for the pizza. She put the leftovers in the refrigerator as I trotted off to my room. I hurriedly dialed Tami from my contact list.

"What happened?" I asked when she answered.

"Oh Michelle! Where have you been?" She sounded exactly as I imagined. Panic mode. She wasn't crying or anything, but angry. Tami was always one to be more enraged than sad when someone hurt her.

"Mom took me to The Pizzeria."

"You kidding me? Anyway, Sean broke our date! What's worse is the way he did it! By text message!"

What guy would break a date with someone over text? I thought. "I guess he's not a real man since he couldn't tell you face to face," I said.

"Yeah and he didn't even try to call me!"

"So that was it?" I asked, sitting on my bed and kicking off my ankle boots. "No reason why?"

"Nope."

"All right," I said. "Tami I have to tell you something."

"What is it? Do you know something about him? Do you know something about his job? Is he really poor?"

"Slow down!" I couldn't believe she was worried about this guy's income of all things. "He is married."

"WHAT?!"

Her voice pierced my eardrum. "Calm down!" I said.

"How do you know?"

I cleared my throat. "Before you have a conniption, someone else went and looked at the house. He asked Sean if he had a girlfriend and Sean said no, that he had a wife." I hoped I remembered it correctly.

"Who was it? You said he! The only he that you talk to is Brad!" She yelled.

"Yes it is him, but don't be going and saying anything!" I raised my voice, not even thinking about Mom hearing me.

"Why did you do that? Why did you have to go into the house again?"

"I didn't go in! And does it matter? He is married, Tami!"

She paused, taking a deep breath. "So is that why he broke the date?"

I lowered my voice. "How do I know? It's possible. I mean, his wife probably had something going on with him. Maybe she was originally going away and then decided to stay home so he was stuck with her."

"Yeah!" She sounded more positive now. "It could be that he couldn't call me because she was, like, home, so that's the reason for the text. How do you know all of this?"

"I don't know if that's why he texted you."

"Oh, it probably was. Thanks for the talk! You are the best!" She was giddy again like at school.

"Are you okay now?"

"Oh yeah," she said, laughing. "I just wish I was as smart as you."

"I just observe a lot watching TV. This stuff happens all the time on there. What I don't get is you act like it's okay that he is married. What about his wife?"

"What do you mean?"

I was stunned. I never saw this side of Tami. She was definitely blindsided. "Don't you care that he is married?"

"You just said this stuff happens all the time."

"Yeah, on TV! That doesn't mean it's gotta happen to you! You are the other woman!" I was flabbergasted. She was acting like nothing was wrong with this.

"Luanne did it too!" she said.

"Yeah, and now she is missing!" I reminded her. "It may have been him she was messing with."

"That's just a rumor. Anyway, I will talk to you tomorrow. See you at school."

She was ending the call just like that. I had more to discuss with her, but obviously I wasn't getting through.

"Okay," I said. "Bye."

That was the end of the conversation. I wasn't going to sleep any time soon. I laid awake and tried to imagine Tami as a married man's girlfriend. She had to get her head on straight. I had a feeling this would end horribly.

Just then a text came in from Brad. I smiled, happy to hear from him. The text read: Michelle, Betty is the goofy Broadway actress Nichols was talking about. Google her name.

I was confused at first. "Goofy Broadway actress?" I said out loud. Then it dawned on me. I got out of bed and booted up my computer while texting Brad back.

What is her last name? I asked him by text.

I thought it would be easier if I searched for her first and last name instead of Guardian Angels. His reply read: Fitzgerald. I thanked him by text and clicked on the internet icon. I didn't really have anything to accomplish, but I thought I could see what Betty looked like.

The Guardian Angels site came up when I searched her name. I clicked on the link to the website and saw her photo. She had blonde, almost white hair, perfectly straight with an under flip. Her teeth were about as white as her hair. She was wearing a red blazer with a white turtleneck blouse underneath. I also found that she was a representative offering her phone number and email for people who want to foster, adopt, or become a mentor. I read about mentoring which meant someone was able to take a child to the movies, zoo, or outdoor group activities.

I wondered if Luanne did that, but then again, Katie and Deedee lived with her. I was curious about the site, so I clicked on the Find A Child link. I was disappointed that no names or photos came up. I typed in Katie Brashers. Nothing. I just saw a message to email or call a representative to set up a time for an interview.

I felt that we were at a dead end. It crossed my mind that Luanne kidnapped the girls and ran off to Florida, but then Betty would have asked Brad more questions about what he knew or who he was. Also, the police would have been all over a kidnapping. No, kidnapping was definitely out of the question.

Betty Fitzgerald and a phone number with email is all we had. It crossed my mind to email her, but I had no idea what to say. I was afraid it would cause more harm than good. I didn't want to get caught doing something I wasn't supposed to. Tami would be all over this if we had a reason to email the agency. Email is better in a sense that no voices could be heard, but then they could trace email addresses back to where they are routed from. This happened to someone at school who played a prank on someone.

I went on to bed, lying awake, thinking about Brad and if he was still plugging away at his computer.

Chapter 17

Tami was cheerful the next morning, but then she did a total reversal that afternoon. She was bummed that Sean never called back.

"What is wrong with him?" she asked me before accounting class, as if I knew. "His wife can't be with him this entire time!" She was panicking again.

"Tami, lower the voice, please!" I told her. "This is wrong anyway. You don't need to be dating him."

"Oh, okay Miss Holier Than Thou! I am really hurt here and you act like I should just give up!" Her voice became louder.

I hollered back, "You should never have gotten started! You have no business with a guy that age anyway!"

"I can't deal with you anymore! I don't get why he hasn't called and you don't care!" She was almost insulting me with her eyes with the way she was glaring at me. Tami had never looked at me that way.

I stopped and turned to see everyone standing, staring at us. Then I turned around to look into the classroom where my classmates were also staring.

"Let's go to class," I whispered.

"No!" Tami said. "I'm going to the office. I don't feel well!" She stormed off.

I walked into Ms. Runyon's class with all eyes on me. You could hear a pin drop, it was so quiet.

"Michelle," Ms. Runyon said. "Everything okay with Tami?"

Shaking my head, I sat at my desk. "She's sick. Going to the office."

Ms. Runyon flipped the switch on the intercom speaker.

"Yes?" The secretary said.

"Tami Simmons is on her way to the office," Ms. Runyon told her. "Let me know if she doesn't show."

"Sure thing!" she answered.

"Okay, let's get to work!" She clapped her hands once as if she were excited. "I know it's Friday, so I'm not going to be too harsh on homework. I also think you deserve a break since everyone worked so hard on their balance sheets. You did work hard, didn't you?"

Some people nodded while others just stared blank faced. I didn't know how I did. I rushed through my homework the best I could so I hoped I did well.

"Balance sheets to the front please! Chop chop people!"

I laughed to myself at her attitude and retrieved mine from my folder. I turned to collect Brad's while he looked at me with a strange eye. Almost like he wanted to say something to me. I couldn't tell if he was mad or just confused.

"Thanks," I said, taking his paper.

After class was over, Brad stopped me at my desk.

"Hey, I'm sorry I got mad at you." He had his head down, apologetically.

"Oh, that's okay." What a relief! I was happy he finally talked to me. "It was my fault. I didn't think before I spoke out loud like that. Oh, and thanks for texting me last night about Betty."

"I was thinking," he was fidgeting with his hands, "would you wanna go out tonight?"

"Really?" I was overwhelmed. I could not believe Brad Wilkes was actually asking me out! My face was heating up. "Sure!" But then I thought I would have to tell Mother. I would do that at the salon.

"Okay." He smiled. "I was thinking of going to Equalizer. I've never been there."

"You haven't?" This came as a shock since every student in the area had been to the under twenty-one club, but then again I didn't remember seeing him there.

"No. I never had anyone to go with. Katie never wanted to go, or Luanne never let her."

"Okay, well, I'm getting my hair done later. How about seven?" It just came out naturally since Tami and I always went at that time. Then it dawned on me that Tami might want to go. What do I do now? I thought. Oh well, I'll worry about that later.

"That'll work," he said. "I'll swing by and pick you up."

I nodded, grinning from ear to ear. It didn't matter to

me who would see us there or what my mom would say. I was enjoying this short moment while I had it.

Science class didn't go as well. Mr. Beaverton wasn't impressed with the work we handed in. Some did great since science came naturally to the smart kids who were programmed to learn anything, even something as boring as science. Some of us weren't that lucky. At least he didn't assign any homework which made a better weekend for me. I hoped the rest of the weekend turned out this well.

Tami was on the bus when I got on. I walked to our seat while she glared up at me.

"You wanna sit with me, huh?"

"Yeah, why wouldn't I?" I could not get over her attitude. So what if I thought messing around with a married man was wrong. Didn't everybody?

She moved her backpack off of the seat so I could sit. "Fine!" she said.

"So did you sit in the office that whole time?" I asked.

"Yeah! Where did you think I went?"

I shrugged. "I dunno. I thought maybe you were trying to get a hold of Sean."

"Oh, I will get a hold of him all right!"

I took this as just talk. Tami always ran her mouth without realizing what she was saying. "My mom asked if you wanted to go to the movies with us tomorrow night," I said, dodging the subject of Sean. I was hoping to put her in a better mood.

"I will let you know," she said, pouting. "I don't know if

I'm up to seeing a movie."

"My dad's coming home. It will be nice if you would join us."

Her eyes softened. She smiled a little. "Well, I might."

"I am sorry about everything," I told her. "You will find your Mr. Right."

"Michelle, Mr. Right needs to be found immediately."

I didn't know what she was talking about. "What do you mean, immediately?" I had a thought that maybe she was pregnant, but didn't know of her having sex with anyone.

"Meaning, he could be out there," she pointed her thumb to the window as the bus started moving. "Do you know people find the right guy early in life? I don't wanna wait around and finally settle with someone when I'm thirty and old. I want the right one now."

I didn't care how she was going to react with my next statement. "Tami, I think you were interested in Sean for his money."

"Yeah so?"

"You are not in love with him. You barely know him and he has no idea you are sixteen."

She was quiet after that as she turned to the window. Nothing else was said on our way home.

Chapter 18

Around four o'clock, Mom called and said the shop was clear. I drove Dad's car since she didn't want to lock up the place to come get me.

When I got there, she had her hands on her hips. "You ready?" she asked, her eyes narrowing.

"Yeah, what's wrong?" I dropped my purse into the next chair. I could still smell the hair spray and treatments that were used through the day.

"Sit!" she demanded. She started combing my hair in sections. "Well?"

"Well what?" I asked. I was worried that she found out about the book.

"I hear you have been seeing someone."

My heart almost stopped. I knew this place was full of gossip. "What do you mean, seeing someone?"

"Katie's boyfriend! You know who I am talking about!" She combed my hair hard, pulling my head back with every stroke.

"Mom, he is just a friend from school. What's the big

deal? Katie is gone now."

"Well, he sure doesn't waste time, does he?" She swung my chair around so I was facing her. "Michelle, why didn't you tell me?"

I just looked at her. I couldn't get over the remark she just made about Brad. She was judging him already. A line formed between her eyes. I hated it when she looked like this. She reminded me of an evil queen in a fairy tale.

"I'd like to know if you are seeing a boy behind my back."

"Behind your back? I see him at school. Who told you this anyway?"

"You don't worry about who told me." She pointed at me with the comb.

"I haven't seen him socially." Now was my chance if any. "But he did ask me out for tonight."

"Oh, so you were gonna go behind my back?"

"No, mom! I was going to tell you about it."

"When?"

"Here, while I was getting my hair done."

"Well, I had to hear it from some random customer!"

I knew she heard about this at work. "I was going to say something about him, but I haven't dated yet. I didn't know how you felt about it."

"You are sixteen! It's about time you got asked out sometime this year."

She swung me back around and continued combing.

"Ouch!" I said.

She stopped and took a deep breath. "Okay, I'm sorry. I just want you to tell me things. This is something a daughter is supposed to tell her mother."

"I didn't think anything would happen with this guy. He just asked me out today. Did this person tell you that too?" I asked, looking at her through the mirror.

She shook her head. "No, she didn't. With the way she talked, it was as if you already had went out."

I laughed. "No Mom. We haven't."

"Okay, I jumped to conclusions." She grabbed the brush to slather my hair. "Sorry I flew off the handle."

"It's okay."

"But, I want to meet him. Where is he taking you?"

"Equalizer."

"Again? Don't you and Tami go there?"

"Yeah, but he has never been there."

"Mmmm," was all she said, continuing with my highlights.

The rest of my salon visit went smoothly. Mother talked about my school work and later about Dad making it home that night. She was hoping she would be up to greet him. I apologized again for not telling her about Brad before I left. She seemed much better, but I wished she wouldn't freak out the way she does. There were times when I wondered if she should be on medication.

Chapter 19

Iwas getting ready for my date when Dad arrived at six-thirty. I heard his semi pull up in our driveway.

Mom shouted from the living room, "Michelle! Daddy's home!" like I was a little kid. I came out of my room with a blush brush in my hand.

"Oh, if I would have known he was gonna get home this early, I would have cooked dinner!"

"Mom, I'm sure he won't care. You can always whip up a fast pasta dinner."

"That's true! I do have spaghetti!" She was acting like a teenager. I found it ironic that I was the one supposed to be acting this way before my date.

"Hi honey!" she said excitingly when he got one foot in the door. She threw her arms around him.

He didn't respond since his hands were full. "Hey there," he greeted. "I'm so tired."

"Here." I went to him and grabbed his cooler, thermos, and duffel bag.

"Thanks honey," he told me.

Mom drew herself away from him, straightening up her shirt. "Sorry," she said. "I just missed you."

He made his way in and plopped down on the couch. "Boy!" he said to me. "You look stunning!"

"Oh, I'm just getting ready to go out."

I had my black button up sleveless blouse on with a pair of black jeans. I also wore my black ankle boots. I was skeptical about wearing black in spring, but if it worked for Tami, I though it would work for me. Mom blow dried my hair while using a round brush so it was bouncy and felt so soft.

"She has a date!" Mom said excitingly.

"First one?" he asked.

I nodded. "Do I look too formal?"

"Oh, no!" he shook his head. "Black is best to wear at night! Very classy!"

I laughed. I never thought of myself as classy.

"I have to finish getting ready." I leaned over and kissed him. "Nice to have you home."

"Oh, it's nice to be home, little one!"

He always called me that. I didn't like it, but would never tell him.

I finished up just as a knock came at the door.

"Oh, Michelle!" Mom called from the living room again.

I emerged to find Brad talking to my parents. I was glad they met on their own so I wouldn't have had to introduce them, being all nervous as I was.

Brad looked good in a dark green v-neck shirt and blue jeans. He was more casual, but it didn't matter. I was happy to be the one overdressed instead of the other way around.

"Wow!" he said, his face lighting up when he saw me. "You look great!"

"My salon touch!" Mom said beaming. "Isn't she beautiful?"

Is this my mother? I thought. She never used those words to describe me. I didn't even know that word was in her vocabulary.

He nodded, looking at my dad as if he was afraid to be too happy upon seeing me.

"Well, have fun kids," Dad said. "We will wait up."

Brad gave a nervous laugh.

We talked mostly about Luanne and Katie while on the road. The ride was smooth even though it felt like we were sunk down, riding on the ground. A musk scented air freshener dangled from the rearview mirror.

"I feel we are at a dead end," he told me, adjusting his mirror.

"I was afraid of that too," I confessed. "I don't know much about adoption or anything."

"Me neither, but I'm surprised that Luanne would be able to just move the girls away if she wasn't their legal guardian." He never took his eyes off the road.

"How do you know she wasn't?"

"They had different last names, Michelle."

"Oh, yeah," I said, hoping I didn't sound stupid. I

wasn't thinking straight.

"Shoot, they could be in someone else's care by now if they didn't go to Florida."

I thought about that for the rest of our ride to Equalizer. If someone else had Katie, there would be no way of finding her or my book. Not to mention she had my cell phone number, so I thought she would call me if she was able to.

When we arrived, many cars were pulling up with kids pouring out. Some had their parents let them off down the road so they wouldn't be embarrassed in front of the kids who had a car. I wondered how everyone would react to seeing me with Brad. I was actually here with a date! Just then my phone went off. Tami was texting me. I ignored it as I started to get out of the car.

"Wait," Brad said, grabbing my arm.

"Yeah?"

"Your parents seem really nice and I'm glad I got to meet them, but this isn't really a date."

Oh no, I thought. Here it comes. I figured this was too good to be true. Why would someone like Brad even want to be seen with ordinary me? But then, Katie was ordinary too.

"What do you mean? You asked me to come. I didn't even get money from Mom and Dad." I felt a panic coming on, but I did my best to remain cool on the surface.

"Oh no, I'll pay for it. I mean, I'm not looking for a girlfriend right now. I just wanted to go out and have fun. I'm still upset over Katie and all. I guess I'm hoping she comes back."

I nodded, but in that instant, jealousy stabbed me. I resented Katie more than I ever did at that point. We had been friends, but Brad still wanted her. Katie and I were parallel. Our personalities, goals and even our physiques were similar. So, what was wrong with me? Why couldn't he be interested in me when I was right there in front of him?

"I understand," I said even though I really didn't mean it.

"Good!" He said with a big smile. "Now, let's go party!"

What a bummed night, I thought. I could have just come with Tami.

I was wondering if she would be mad at me for going out without her. I went ahead and read her text when we got to the door. She asked what I was doing. I texted back that I was out with Brad and left it at that. She answered with a sad face made up with a colon and parenthesis.

We got our sodas and sat at the bar. The music was pounding in my ears. I usually enjoyed it, but I wasn't feeling it this time. The cold crisp taste of my cola helped me feel a little better, but I was still hurt.

"Oh, well look at this!" A bimbo type voice said.

I turned to find Tiffany standing there twisting her long blonde, almost white locks into a spiral with one hand. Her clique stood on both sides of her.

"Yeah, what?" I asked firmly.

"You just dove right in didn't you?" she said to Brad as her friends laughed falsely. "Looks like we have the two suspects right here!"

"What are you talking about?" Brad asked, standing from his stool.

"Boy, you don't shop around, do you?" she said. "Maybe you two had this whole thing planned from the start." She looked at me up and down. "Talk about taking a step down."

It was then that I snapped. I couldn't take it anymore. I jumped off the bar stool and grabbed her shoulders before Brad had a chance to stop me. "I HAD IT WITH YOU AND YOUR SPIRAL BARBIE DOLL HAIR! YOU CAN JUST GO TO HELL!" I gave her hair a hard yank and tried to mess it up as best as I could.

The other girls' mouths dropped.

"This style is out dated by the way, bitch!" I pushed her hard, her back hitting the wall behind her. I then sat back down and tried to cool off.

Tiffany looked like she was going to cry. "By the way," she said. "Hope you got a good look at that house!"

I jumped up again and they all three ran off as fast as their high heels would allow. One of them stumbled and almost fell.

"Where did that come from?" Brad asked with amazement. "That was great!"

"Nowhere," I told him. "Just sick of them. It's been coming for a long time."

"Man, you are all red faced!" he said. "You okay?"

I nodded as I slowed my breathing.

"How do they know we were in that house?" he asked.

"They could be making it up. Someone could have seen me talking to you in the car and assumed we were there." I didn't put anything past Tiffany. She made up stories at the drop of a hat.

"Maybe," he said.

"And no, this isn't me living in a candy land world!" I spat back at him.

"What do you mean?"

"You know, what you said to me in your car about that."

"Oh," he looked apologetic. "I'm sorry. I didn't mean anything by it. I just know there's got to be an explanation for Katie's disappearance." I nodded.

"You wanna go soon?" he asked.

I shrugged. "It doesn't matter. I'm not much in a party mood tonight." What a waste of a nice hair style, I thought.

We talked more about the house and Sean. We both knew there was no way we could ever get back in the house after he saw both of us. The only link we had was Tami and I wasn't sure how she would react to seeing him again.

"There's no way I would ask her to do that again," I told him. "It's too risky anyway."

"Yeah," was all he said.

"I guess we will have to just wait and see what happens or if anyone around town hears from one of them."

He looked over at me. "You giving up?"

"No, I just don't know what else to do."

"I'm not giving up," he said flatly. "I can't get in the house again either, but I won't just give up."

"I'm not giving up!" I raised my voice at whatever he was implying. "We will have to think of something else if you wanna search this any more. Like emailing Betty."

"About what?" he asked loudly, over the music. He was getting excited and not in a good way. "Wanting to adopt a kid?" His eyes narrowed.

"I don't know, I just thought about it when I was looking up the agency on the internet."

"That's outta the question," he said, taking a drink of his soda.

"I'm sorry Brad. I wish I could come up with something." I told him. I didn't want to end this night in an argument.

"That's okay, I know how hard it is. It's not like we were ever allowed in her house all that much."

"I never was," I reminded him.

After a few more minutes, we decided to go home. It was a quiet ride home and we just said goodbye when he dropped me off. I sent Tami a text apologizing for not texting or calling her any more that night.

Mom and Dad were in bed, but not asleep. "Michelle, is that you?" Mom called.

"Yeah, tired. Going to bed."

"You okay, honey?" Dad called.

"Yeah, everything is fine."

I went to my room and laid down. Tami never answered my message. Buster started whining at my door. I let him in as he walked straight to my bed and jumped up on it. I got back under the covers and nuzzled him, crying myself to sleep.

Chapter 20

I laid awake in bed the next morning, thinking about my life. What was I here for? Brad didn't care that much about me and Tami was upset that I was out last night. I felt as if I dumped my best friend for some guy who didn't even care about me. What was I thinking?

Either Mom or Dad came in to let Buster out of my room while I was asleep. At ten o'clock, my phone vibrated. I got up and grabbed it from my dresser. It was Tami.

The text read: Sorry I didn't answer you last night. I went out to find Sean.

I called her right away. "What do you mean you went out to find him?" I asked when she answered.

"I wasn't spending a Friday night in!" she said. "Why didn't you tell me about Brad?"

"I dunno." I should have told her. I knew it was a mistake not to since we were best friends.

"Aren't you still my friend?" she asked, her voice cracking.

"Yes Tami, of course I am! Now, what did you do?"

"Well, I drove to his house. First I drove to the rental house and parked behind it, on Cedar. I thought about throwing something through a window. I didn't know what else to do to make him mad. Then he pulled up to the house."

"And?" I said, wanting more.

"Some other car pulled in after his. I could only see part of the driveway from my angle, so I got out of the car and walked up to the house."

"What happened? You didn't knock, did you?"

"No, I could see through one of the kitchen windows. I thought he was showing some guy the house but they kept talking about a business deal."

"Like what?"

"I dunno. How would I know? They just mentioned money alot. I never heard an amount, but Sean was asking for it. I ended up following him when he left."

"Wonder what that was," I said. "Rent or something? Maybe he found a renter." I hoped this person wouldn't move in, find my book and sell it, if it was still in the house somewhere. "Did you see the guy?"

"Just some blondish hair. I didn't wanna look all the way in, in case they saw me." She had an edge to her voice. "Want me to get to the main point here?"

"Fine!" I said, not happy with her tone. "Where did you follow him to?"

"His house in Marian." she said. "Mr. Upscale on Breckenridge Lane. I knew he had money."

"Yeah, and?"

"I sat outside, watching him go into the house. Then I, like, saw his wife through the window, sitting in a chair watching television. Looks like a big flat screen on the wall."

I hoped she wasn't going to tell me what they were watching.

"He sat on the couch."

"So?"

"So, that means they aren't close at all. If they were close, she would have, like, sat with him. She looks like crap anyway. He can do so much better."

I rolled my eyes. "Okay Tami, what happened? Did you knock on the door or anything?"

"Well, no. I found out where he lives at least."

"And now what?"

"I dunno!" She sounded defensive. "Sorry not to have an interesting story. Maybe you have a better one from last night!"

"No, Tami I don't. Nothing happened, but I did yell at Tiffany when we were at Equalizer."

"Tiffany?" She laughed. "I wish I would have seen that! Wait, you went to Equalizer? Without me?"

"Calm down," I told her. "Brad had never been there since Katie never wanted to go, so he wanted to see what it was like."

"Katie never did anything. Is he still stuck on her or something?"

I sighed. "Yeah, it looks like it."

"So now what?"

"I don't know, but I'm not wasting time with someone who doesn't want me."

There was a pause between us and I realized what I'd said. I had sounded more like the way Tami should be feeling about Sean.

"By the way," I said, changing the subject, "Tiffany knows we were in the house."

"WHAT?" she gasped.

"I know," I said. "It better not get back to our parents or I will continue what I said to her."

"I so wish I would have seen that!"

"I should have went out with you instead last night. I'm sorry I didn't call you to have you meet us there."

"Don't worry about it. We have been, like, friends for life, haven't we? Why let this little mishap get in the way?"

We laughed and talked a little more. I asked her about going to the movies again and she agreed to join us. We got off the phone and I felt much better. The day looked brighter as if I had something to look forward to. I decided to get up and get dressed. I wanted to visit with Dad.

"Are you doing okay?" Mom asked as I entered the kitchen. The smell of hazelnut filled the room. She was still in her nightgown, reading the paper over coffee.

"Yeah, where's Dad?"

"He left to go to the store. He wanted to pick up steaks to have out on the grill."

I'd missed our cookouts. We hadn't had one in so long. I went to the cupboard to get the box of toaster pastries and popped two in the toaster.

"Why did you ask me if I was doing okay?"

"I thought I heard you crying last night."

"Yeah, Brad isn't as great as I thought," I said reluctantly.

"Oh, you had a crush on him, huh?" she smiled.

"Mother!" I said laughing.

"It's okay! I had those too when I was your age."

"You did?" I was surprised. I never saw Mom as a guy chaser.

"Yes crushes existed in the dinosaur days too, ya know."

I laughed out loud. "I just didn't know you did that, that's all." I leaned my elbows on the counter top. How I loved these talks.

"What? I went to school too, ya know! Actually," she put her paper down, "I had the biggest crush when I was older. It was on a classmate in beauty school."

"What?" I jumped back from the counter.

"It was a guy, Michelle!" She knew what I was thinking.

For a minute I was spooked. "Whew, okay."

"Well, he turned out to be, you know."

"Gay?"

She laughed. "Yeah, that. What a disappointment. I cried for weeks."

"How did you get through it?"

"We just stayed friends and he helped me though many of our exams. We did hair and got tested on it. He showed me a lot of tips."

"That's nice," I said.

"You can still remain friends even if the person isn't interested in anything more, Michelle."

I nodded. "I know." The pastries popped up and I took them out, almost burning my fingers.

I sat down and ate at the table. The chocolate was so hot it tasted exactly like hot fudge melting in my mouth. The sprinkles on top were like candy.

Mom started talking about the movies listed in the paper. We were pretty open about seeing anything that was showing. We didn't get many movie nights out so anything was a possibility.

After I finished up, I grabbed Buster's leash from the wall hook.

"Okay Boy, you ready?"

He jumped off the couch and hurried to me with his short legs, his ears swaying back and forth.

"Thanks for being there for me, Bud," I said, patting his head after snapping on his leash. He was a big comfort to me the night before. I loved Buster as a member of the family and hoped he lived a long time.

It was a warm day. I could feel summer just around the corner which meant school was going to be out soon. I loved it when school was out. I never had to worry about grades or seeing people like Tiffany everyday.

I walked Buster up the road and passed by the rental house. It looked like flowers were planted in the front yard by the walkway. Yellow and red ones were alternated.

Very cute, I thought. Sean must be wanting this place to look more appealing.

I wanted to take a closer look at them so I tugged on Buster's leash and walked up the driveway.

The flowers released a heavenly fragrance. I didn't know what they were, but they gave the house a more homey look. Buster stuck his nose in and I pulled him back.

"No, you don't eat those!" I told him.

We walked by the flowers and Buster squatted. I looked around to make sure nobody saw that he was dropping a present in the yard. It's not like anyone lived there anyway. He always did this at home.

"Hurry up, Boy," I told him.

After doing his business, he led me around the side of the house.

"Oh, okay," I said, hesitating.

Curiosity got the best of me. I couldn't look in the windows because of the blinds being pulled shut, so we went into the backyard. At first, I just looked around. Nothing was in the backyard but a swing set. I forgot to ask Sean if that was his mother's too. It seemed unlikely to me that an old woman would have one of those. I playfully pushed one of the swings back and forth, remembering what it was like to swing in one. I then sat down in it to get a feel of my childhood. Buster just looked at me strangely, then started pulling me toward the center of the yard.

"Okay, Buster! Gimme a minute!"

I got up and looked over at Mr. Nichols's house. He

wasn't outside. I hoped he didn't see me over here, but I wasn't doing any harm.

Just then, Buster started sniffing the ground. It wasn't regular behavior for him to be sniffing this fast. He was walking and stopped abruptly, touching his nose to a spot in the yard. It was an area where new grass looked as if it was starting to grow. I remembered Sean saying something about planting grass seed back here.

"Buster, what is it?" I asked him as if he was going to answer me.

Then he started digging with his paws.

"Buster!" I yelled. "Stop that!" I tried to pull on his leash, but he kept going. His paws were like tires on a race car, speeding to the finish line. He was kicking up dirt behind him and it was hitting my sneakers. "There's no bone in there!" I didn't know what he was looking for or thought was in the ground. Then I smelled something foul.

"Oh my God!" I said loudly. The smell about knocked me over. I tugged on Buster's leash again. "COME ON!" I yelled. He responded to my tone.

"Hey!" I heard Mr. Nichols call.

I turned and saw him waving. I ran toward the street.

"Mr. Nichols, call the police! There's something over here in the yard!" I was panicking so bad, I forgot I had my phone in my back pocket. I sat down by the side of the road and took deep breaths. The next thing I knew, the sound of police sirens were off in the distance, coming closer.

Chapter 21

I didn't realize I was shaking until the police arrived. The first thing I remembered was an officer talking to me. I raised my head and all I could make out was a figure, blinded by the glare of the sun.

"Who are you?" he asked.

"She lives just down the road!" I heard Mr. Nichols call from across the street. "She told me to call ya'all."

"Okay," the officer called back. "What is your name hon?" he asked me.

"Um, Michelle," I said slowly, shielding my eyes with my hand. "Michelle Martin."

All of a sudden, I noticed my mother in the yard.

"What is going on?" she demanded. "What is my daughter doing here?"

The officer went to her and said something but I couldn't hear him. She then stomped over toward me. Buster was whining.

"Why of all places would you come here?" she asked, furiously. "I told you to stay away from this place!"

KELLI SUE LANDON

"Buster-"

"Oh, blame the dog! Real smooth, Michelle! You expect me to believe that?"

I couldn't see what was going on in the yard where we smelled the horrific odor.

"Buster found something, Mom!" I said. I didn't know why she was so upset. If something was buried here, we did the right thing. At least I thought.

"I don't care! Get your ass home young lady!"

How embarrassing. I was sure Mr. Nichols was watching this, not to mention any other neighbors who could see into the backyard. They were all outside, gawking with their hands on their foreheads, stretching to see past the sunlight.

"Ma'am," the officer called. "We need to take her in."

My heart stopped. What was he talking about? Was I going to jail?

"She did nothing wrong!" Mom persisted.

"No, she didn't. She did everything right. We need to question her. We don't know who this is yet, but she might know the person."

"Person?" Mom put a hand over her open mouth. "Oh, dear God!" she said, almost a whisper.

"Just go to the police station. We will meet you there," the officer instructed. "You can bring the dog."

"And if we don't?" she asked sternly.

"You will be interferring with a case which means you would be arrested."

She gasped. "Michelle! How could you?" She put her hands on her hips.

"No need to be mad at her ma'am."

"The name is Nancy!" she demanded.

"Okay Nancy, your daughter did the right thing. You should be proud."

"It was Buster," I whispered to Mom. "He is the hero. Not me."

"Let's go!" she said, grabbing my arm. I had just realized I still had a hold of Buster's leash.

We arrived at the station where we had to wait for what seemed like hours, but was only forty-five minutes according to Mother. She was pacing the floor and chugging so many cups of coffee, I lost count after number four. The place was filled with phones ringing in my ears and chattering all around. I could not stand to work in a place like this.

A strange looking guy sat against the wall across the room, staring at us. I wondered if his mother ever scolded him about his green mohawk and the tattoos on his face.

"I called your dad," Mom informed me. "There is no need for him to come down here, but I wanted to let him know where we were."

"What did he say?" I asked.

"He was more stunned than anything since we don't know what this thing is about." She finally stopped pacing.

"Mom, I'm worried," I told her. Buster whined at my feet.

Bending down to face me, her look softened somewhat. She took my chin in her hand. "Look, I'm sorry about how I reacted."

This was a relief. I hoped she would ease up on me.

"What is it you are worried about? The officer said you did nothing wrong." she stood back up and took another drink of coffee.

"I'm worried about what they found. What if it's Luanne or Katie?"

"Michelle, don't worry about what they found until they tell you."

"Didn't that cross your mind?"

She sat next to me and patted Buster's head to ease his whining. "It did actually. I mean Luanne's reputation wasn't all that clean around town."

I started to cry. "Oh, Mom what if it is? What if it's Katie? What if more bodies are buried in that yard?"

She hugged me and stroked my hair. That felt good. I smelled the sweet fragrance of her body lotion which soothed me even more.

"Do you know how bad that smell was?" I asked her.

"Well, I've never smelled a dead body, but I have had my share of bad meat in the fridge and I hear it's a lot like that."

"If that's how meat smells when it goes bad, I'm becoming a vegetarian!"

She let out a small laugh. "No, we are having steaks

with Dad later, remember?"

I wondered if there was anybody else who knew this had happened. I also thought about what Tami or Brad would say when they found out. How would Brad take it? He would be crushed hearing of Luanne or Katie maybe being dead. I buried my face in my hands, thinking about it.

"Michelle, calm down. That officer better be coming or Mother is going to go into one of her rages!" she said loudly.

Just then the officer showed up to take us into a room. I stood and wiped my wet hands on my jeans.

We sat at a table while he introduced himself. I saw him better now. He was very attractive with coal black hair and mocha colored skin.

"I'm Officer Avalos," he said, putting a note pad down on the table and flipping it open.

"Oh, I thought you had a touch of an accent," said Mother. "Very nice!" She flipped her jet black hair back off her shoulder.

I couldn't believe it! I thought. She was flirting!

"Yes, well let's get to the matter at hand please," he said. "Michelle, you wanna explain to me what happened?"

I told him everything I could. About the walk, the flowers, Buster going to the bathroom, then leading me around the backyard. I felt like an idiot telling him I sat on the swing. He wrote in his pad as I talked.

"Now you were classmates with the former resident, correct?"

"Yeah," I said. "It was Katie. Deedee was the little one."

Mom patted my knee as if to tell me to shut up. I didn't know if that's what she meant, but it seemed like it. I was nervous and I wanted to go home. I would give them anything they wanted at that point.

"And were you ever in the house?"

"No," I said. "Katie wasn't allowed to have friends inside."

He looked at me like he was amazed. "So, you have never ever been inside that house, correct?"

I thought of Tami taking me inside to look at it. What if they talked to Sean and he told them about us saying we wanted to rent it out? "Um, well." Mom stared at me intently. "I was in there when it was up for rent."

"WHAT?!" Mom hollered out."

Buster, startled at her voice, jumped up from his nap.

"Ma'am, please!" he told her.

I felt my face flush. "Sean showed us the place."

"Showed you and who else?"

I was trapped. I didn't mean to say the word, us. I hated to bring anyone else into this, but I had no choice. "My friend Tami."

"Tami, who?" He was jotting things down vigorously now.

"Simmons." I turned to Mom. "Mom, I'm sorry but we wanted to know if we could find anything inside the house that would tell us what happened to them. They all just up and left for Florida and didn't come back. Isn't that odd?"

I wasn't ready to confess about the book.

She just glared at me, shaking her head slowly.

"So, Sean Watson showed you the house. Did he know who you were?"

"Well, we used our real names, but he never knew us." I never told him my last name, but I never lied about it either. I didn't tell him that Tami told Sean we were sisters.

"Did you find anything inside?" he asked.

I shook my head.

"Is that a no?" he asked.

"Yes, no," I said. Betty's phone number didn't matter. I didn't see a reason to mention it.

"And whose idea was this?" Mom asked with a firm tone.

I hesitated then said, "Both of ours." If I said it was Tami's, Mom may not want me hanging around her again. "It was stupid I know."

"Teenagers do stupid things," she said, looking back at Officer Avalos.

Mother was good at humiliating me.

"Did any other friends hang around the house?" he asked.

"Why? Is it Katie?" I was becoming frantic. With these questions, I felt more positive that it was her body.

"We are not able to say yet. I need to know if anyone else hung around the house."

"She had a boyfriend, Brad Wilkes."

He nodded as he wrote.

"Oh, and," I thought it was time to mention Betty since she was in and out of the house. If I didn't, they would question Brad about it or worse, Mr. Nichols. "Brad found out they were a fostered family and some woman named Betty Fitzgerald stopped in all the time."

Mom's eyes widened. "Hmmm," was all she let out.

"How did you know her name?" he asked.

Oh no, now what was I going to say? Mother was making me nervous. "He called her and asked. Then looked up her name on the internet."

Brad was going to freak out on me, I knew it. The officer was sure to ask him how he knew number, but I didn't want to continue talking about it.

"Okay," he said. "I think that's all we need. If we think of anything else, we will call you back in." He started to get up from the table.

"What did you find?" I asked. "Is it Luanne? Katie? Maybe Deedee buried back there?"

"We don't know yet."

"You don't know?" We waited all this time to talk to him and still nothing.

"We cannot say at this time," he said. "The area will be sealed off during the investigation."

"Well, when can you tell who it is?" I asked. "Can't you just look at the person?"

"Yes and no. It's been a dry spring so far which puts us a little closer on identifying the body, but we don't know who specifically this person is. That takes time. We're not *that* good." He let out a chuckle.

Mother's eyes were on me the whole way out of the police station.

I found it hard to believe that they couldn't tell the hair color or age of the dead person. Couldn't they just tell me what they looked like? I thought. It crossed my mind that they could be holding back and not telling us everything.

Chapter 22

After we got home, I went straight to my room. I was going to call Tami, but Dad came in and sat on my bed.

"Don't worry about Mom," he said. "She just hates hearing stories and being questioned while she's at the shop."

I nodded. "I didn't mean for this to happen."

"I know you didn't. It's not your fault. She just knows people are going to say something to her. They might solicit questions instead of giving her their business."

"I know. I just feel bad. I wish I would have never went into that yard."

"Michelle, if you didn't, who knows if the body would have been found this soon?"

I nodded. I did feel good about that part of it.

"We are having steaks for dinner. You still up for a movie?"

I shrugged. "I dunno. I could go with you if you two are still going."

"If you don't feel like it, we understand. It could be like a date night for us." He smiled, rising from the bed.

I retrieved my phone from my pocket and called Tami after he left.

"Hello Michelle!" she said. "What's up?"

"You mean, you haven't heard yet?" I asked.

"Heard what?"

I went through the whole story, ending with what was said at the police station.

"No way!" she said. "They don't know who it is?"

"If they do, they won't tell me. I had to tell them about us looking at the house."

"So?" she said as if it were nothing.

"So, Sean might try to talk to you. He is going to be a big part of this."

"Serves him right," she said.

"Well," I hesitated telling her the next part, "the officer asked me who you were."

"Why? Just because we looked at the house?"

"Yeah, but nothing happened. You just looked at it. You didn't make up a name or anything so I wouldn't worry about it. "

"I wonder who it is! Michelle you really, like, made the news!"

"No, I haven't! I just hope it's not Katie. Or that the others aren't buried in the yard."

"You watch too many movies," Tami said. "It could be anyone. Maybe the body was there before Luanne rented the place."

"Tami, get real! I think it would have been found before

now. The grass was just planted, remember Sean saying that? Buster dug and found it so it wasn't buried very well."

"Maybe the person was in a hurry," She said. "Doesn't sound like it was very planned out."

"Maybe not, but I dunno. I'm sure Brad will be calling. He is gonna be mad as a hornet, probably."

"Who cares if he gets mad? You told the truth!"

"Yeah, I know," I told her. "Thanks for not getting upset."

"It's not your fault, Michelle."

I was happy that she was okay with what I told them. I felt much better so I laid back on my bed and relaxed.

"I don't know if we are still going to the movies tonight."

"That's okay. Maybe you can sleep over," she said.

"I don't see Mom letting me."

"Why?"

I didn't want to bring up the old story of when Tami's brother, Brian, had to babysit us once. When we were little, Brian was around thirteen and he locked us in a closet as a joke. I went crazy, scratching fingernail marks inside the wooden door. Tami's dad actually hit him repeatedly when he saw the door. Mom found out and ever since then, she didn't want me staying over at Tami's for a long period of time. It didn't matter that I grew up and Brian learned his lesson. She never forgot the nightmares I had for months, waking her up in the middle of the night.

"You know how she is." I left it at that, then suggested,

"Maybe you can sleep over here. I have a feeling she isn't gonna want me to leave the house tonight after what happened today."

"Cool! Okay, it's a plan!"

That evening, Mom and I were sitting at the table while Dad was firing up the grill outside. She suggested that Tami come over for dinner.

"We were thinking of having a sleepover here instead of going on the movies if that's okay," I told Mom.

"That's fine with me," she said. "But no leaving the house!"

"Okay." Just as I thought. "Tami was going to bring some movies over anyway." I told her this as I texted Tami to bring clothes with her.

"I mean it!" she said.

"Mom I hope to never go to that house again after all this." I flipped my phone shut. "Don't you think I'm upset over what happened?"

Her expression softened a little. "Yes Honey, I do think that. I know you are upset. I just don't want you getting into any trouble."

"What trouble?" I asked, more concerned than ever about what was rolling around up in her brain.

"Michelle what if whoever did this is watching the house? You may be in danger."

I hadn't thought of that. Just like Mother to get me

worried even more.

"I worry about you," she said. "Next time you walk Buster, take him the other direction."

I nodded. "Okay, I will."

Tami showed up a half hour later with a couple of movies. "I have a love story and a scary story!" she said excitingly.

"Hey Sweetie," Dad greeted her, bringing in the plate of steaks. "How's the old man?"

"Dad? He's always coming home from work and plopping down in the recliner with his beer. He gets tired from lugging around all that mail."

"Scary movie?" I asked her. "How scary?"

"I dunno," she said shrugging. "It might be worth a try. If you get, like, creeped out, we can turn it off."

"Just hope there's no corpses in it."

Mom's head shot up from the table. "Michelle, fix your plate."

"Oh, it was just a funny joke, Nancy." Dad said.

"No joking about what happened! I take it Tami has already heard?"

She nodded, putting down her overnight bag. "Sorry."

"You mean about going into the house, posing as renters?"

Dad snickered. "That was a good one."

Mom glared at him. "What was?"

"They were just acting like detectives, Nancy."

"Well, it's not up to them to find out what happened to Luanne or the girls."

I felt a tremble coming on. "I don't feel like getting up right now."

"I'll bring you a plate," Dad said.

"Sorry Michelle." Mom put her hand on top of mine. "This whole thing just disturbs me. Tami, you can make your plate, dear."

"Sorry about the joke," I told her.

"It's okay. I know some of us have different ways of dealing with things like this." She rose to get a plate for Dad.

I closed my eyes and focused on the smells in the kitchen. Thick grilled mouth watering steaks and hot corn on the cob smelled delicious paired with baked cinnamon apples. I could actually see us outside on a picnic with Buster running after a ball. We were sprawled out on the ground on top of a blanket. I could even smell the cool breeze.

"Michelle?" Tami asked.

I opened my eyes, coming back to reality.

"You looked like you were dreaming," she said laughing.

"I was!" I said with a smile as Dad put my dinner in front of me.

This was going to turn out to be a good night after all. Tami and I watching movies and making popcorn after being stuffed with a dinner that was grilled outside by my dad, the best griller in the neighborhood. I never thought much about Buster's grisly discovery for the rest of the night, until Brad showed up.

Chapter 23

We were startled by a knock at the door.

"Who's that?" Tami asked.

"I dunno." I didn't even hear a car pull up. "Who is it?" I called, grabbing the remote and turning down the television.

"Brad," he answered.

"How do we know it's Brad?" Tami said, making a wisecrack.

"Knock it off, Tami!" he said louder. "Michelle, can you let me in?"

I went to the door and unlocked it. "What is it?" I asked him through the pane in the screen door.

He opened the door and walked in. His eyes were blood shot. "She's dead."

"What?" I asked. "Who?" I wasn't sure if he was talking about Katie or Luanne.

"Katie!" He started bawling, putting his face in his hands.

"Did the police say that? They identified her?" My heart was in my throat. They didn't even call me.

"No they didn't, but I know it's her. It's gotta be!"

I led him over to the couch to sit down. I was appalled that he was speculating like this. "Brad, don't go around saying that! You scared me to death!" I took deep breaths. It took everything I had to keep the shakes from coming back.

"We don't know who it is yet," said Tami, putting down the popcorn bowl.

"Remember Mr. Nichols said they left in an SUV?" I said to him.

We all paused, looking at each other. Luanne came to mind. If the girls left that day, she was the only one left.

"You're right," he said, wiping his eyes. "He did say that, didn't he? He saw them leave the house with suitcases."

"See?" I said. "Don't worry Brad." I hugged him loosely. It just came natural to comfort him, but I let go quickly. "Did they question you?"

He nodded. "Yeah that Mexican guy was asking me all kinds of stuff. I told him the truth, about going in the house and Sean chasing me outta there."

"I wonder if Sean's been questioned," Tami said. "He better be!"

"He was leaving when I got there," Brad told her.

"Did he say anything to you?" she asked. "How did he look? Was he scared?"

"No, he didn't say anything and how do I know if he was scared? He looked like he did before when I saw him. The prick!"

"Yeah, that he is!" Tami said.

"Okay as much as we all like to Sean bash, this isn't helping," I broke in.

"Why didn't you see the body?" Tami asked me. "I mean, why didn't you at least look?"

"Tami, I would have had nightmares for weeks looking at someone buried in the dirt!"

"I wonder if they had a face," she said. "I bet that's why they can't, like, identify the person."

"Stop it!" Brad said, grimacing.

"If they haven't been dead that long, then I'm sure they had something of a face," I told her, rubbing my stomach at the thought of a corpse having no face. "I mean, they just supposedly went to Florida two weeks ago."

"So?" Tami said.

"So, that means if this happened before they left, which I would think it did, they were all alive just before that. Katie and Deedee were in school and Luanne was working at the store."

We all shared a quiet moment.

Then after what seemed like minutes, but was only a few seconds, Tami said what I was thinking. "Luanne."

"You think so?" I asked. I always thought this, but was afraid to say it out loud. It seemed to me as if that made it true.

She nodded.

"I dunno," said Brad. "I dunno what to think."

"You think it was a crime of passion?" asked Tami. "I mean she was, like, supposedly sleeping with a married man."

"Yeah, Sean," I blurted out.

"Maybe she threatened to tell his wife and he snapped," she said, flipping her hair off her forehead. It fell back into the same place. "Her sleeping with him did, like, cross my mind you know!"

I was surprised she suspected him of the affair. "Then why didn't you say anything?"

She shrugged. "I guess I just didn't wanna, like, think of him as a killer."

"That's probably why he broke off your date," I said, pointing to her. "After Brad acting as a renter, he got suspicious."

"Suspicious of what?" Brad asked. "I just asked if he had a girlfriend, or whatever it was I said."

"Right!" I said, now feeling that we were getting closer to the truth. "You were digging too much into his personal life. He may have acted like he was mad at you for coming on to him, but really he was chasing you outta the house because you were asking too many questions about Luanne when she was dead in the backyard."

"I wasn't coming on to him!" he said offensively.

"That's not what I said!" Great, now we were arguing. "Yes you did!"

"Guys, guys, guys!" Tami interrupted. "That's not the issue here!"

"I'm just sayin', I ain't a queer!"

I almost laughed and I could tell Tami wanted to. I couldn't get over the attitude he was taking over this. He was obviously keyed up from being at the police station.

"Yes we all know that," said Tami. "Sean acted like that was the case, but it wasn't."

"Still, he didn't do a very good job burying her if Buster found her," I said.

"Why?" said Brad. "Hounds have noses for that!"

"Well, I never thought of Buster as a professional police dog, okay?"

"Doesn't have to be," Brad said as if he were a dog expert. "Those dogs know their shit."

"Yeah I guess," I said. "Also Sean isn't the type who you would think knows how to bury a body. He's too much of a pencil neck."

"What does that mean?" Tami asked.

"You know, like a geek," I said.

She shook her head and put her hand out as if to stop me from something. "He was a gentleman to me." She looked down at her lap as she added, "I guess that was just a cover, huh?"

"Who cares about that now?" Brad said. "He's a murderer as far as I'm concerned and I will be kicking his ass if he's done something with Katie!"

I could feel the tension in the room. We all wanted to get to the truth. I didn't tell them this, but I thought of going to the police station after school on Monday to tell them what really happened. I just had to figure out a way to do it on my own without Mom finding out.

Chapter 24

Brad left shortly after our conversation. Mom and Dad wouldn't like me having boys over when they were gone.

Tami and I finished the movie, then later talked more about Sean before going to sleep.

"I just don't know if he's, like, capable of that," she said, whispering to me from the floor as I laid in bed.

"Tami you hardly knew him. Anyway, isn't it usually the ones you would least expect?" My mouth was dry from the salty taste the popcorn left in my mouth.

"I guess so. Hey," she bolted upright, "I wonder if he's like, a serial killer."

"I dunno." I was getting tired of assumptions. We knew the truth, so why keep trying to figure it out?

I was going to have to wait until Monday to talk to Officer Avalos. I knew I wouldn't get out of the house with Mom home and with it being a Sunday, he may not be at the station. Not only that, I had to do my homework. I was supposed to write a composition paper about a life changing experience. How ironic was that?

"What's wrong?" Tami asked, still sitting upright on the floor.

"Nothing, just tired." I felt a headache coming on.

"Okay, goodnight," she said, lying back down. "I am glad I never went out with him."

"Me too," I said, yawning. "It was a blessing in disguise."

I contemplated telling her what I was going to do. I would have to sometime, but I made a promise to myself not to until I talked to the police first. I was surprised she didn't ask if I was going to tell them. She never said another word as we drifted into sleep.

The next morning Mom made blueberry pancakes and bacon. If Dad wasn't home, we wouldn't have had a good breakfast like this. Tami was overjoyed by it.

"My mom never cooks," she said, stuffing her mouth with a forkful of pancakes as the maple syrup dripped off her chin.

"Never?" Dad asked her.

After finally chewing what all she had in her mouth, she answered, "Nope. We always order out or have frozen pizza." She took a drink of her juice.

Tami's mom enjoyed owning her own book store better than working for someone. Her father was a postal carrier, in another town, who brought home a good salary. I loved

Tami's parents since they never bore down on her for anything, even grades. How I wished we could change places.

"Poor kids," Mom said trying her best to sound like the World's Greatest Mother. "Well, if you ever wanna come by for dinner, you are more than welcome."

"Thanks," Tami said, shoving another forkful in her mouth.

"Wish I could eat like that again," Mom said with a smile. "Oh, what it's like to be young."

"Yeah," I said sarcastically. "It's great if you don't have to worry about someone on your back for doing a good deed." Did I say that out loud? I thought.

"Excuse me?" Mom said, holding her fork in mid air.

"Michelle!" Dad interjected.

"Sorry," I said looking down, moving a piece of pancake around in the maple syrup with my fork. I got tired of her acting all nice in front of people when I knew how she was most of the time. "Just still upset about yesterday."

"We all are," said mom, her tone hardening.

"I'm more upset with how you treated me when you came up to the house."

"You're still on that?" she said, banging her fork down on her plate. "I thought this was over with."

"No mom," I told her. "It still hurts." My throat had a tinge of soreness as my voice cracked. I was on the verge of crying which I didn't want to do in front of everyone. "You hurt me by telling me to get my ass home, as you put it. Then at the police station, you were more concerned with us going into the house as renters than you were about my safety or the body in the ground!"

Nobody said anything for a few seconds. They all sat there like statues. Mom with her mouth agape finally spoke, "I am sorry Michelle! I told you I was wrong."

I shook my head, trying to see through my watery eyes. "No you didn't."

"Well, I was! I should have been more concerned with you. I'm sorry, okay?"

This was the best apology I was going to get. I guess an apology with an edgy tone is better than none, I thought. "Well, could you at least hear me out before jumping to conclusions from now on?"

She nodded reluctantly. "Yeah, that's fair." She then continued to eat.

I quickly wiped my eyes with my hands. Tami reached over and grabbed my hand. She gave me a smile, making me feel better. As much as Tami could be a wild, carefree naïve teen, she was a great friend. She was always there no matter what.

I was glad to get that out of my system. How I wanted to say those words to my mother for quite some time. Now I was curious to see if she would really agree to my request.

Sunday was the day I did my homework. Lazy, boring Sundays. On the other hand, it was nice to have a quiet day for once. Mom and Dad watched television all day. I studied for my science quiz and wrote my composition paper, stopping only for lunch.

"What's your paper about?" Mom asked, taking a bite of her egg salad sandwich.

We were at the kitchen table, but Dad was still watching baseball on TV.

"It's gotta be about a life changing experience."

She almost choked on her sandwich.

"What?" I asked.

She shook her head, grabbing a napkin from the center of the table. "Nothing," she said.

"I'm not writing about that." I told her.

"Well, I would hope not!" Her eyes bulged. "Could you imagine what everyone would say or ask?"

Mother was always worried about what other people thought. Who really cared? I knew she saw almost the whole town come into the shop, but why was this such a big deal? I didn't want to pursue this, so I did my best to think of another topic to write my paper on.

"What about the time you won the spelling bee at school?" she asked.

I was shocked she changed the subject. "Yeah," I said, smiling, holding my sandwich in mid air. "Everyone in the class actually noticed me after that."

"What, were you invisible?"

"Well, there were times when I thought I was."

"More boys noticed you, you mean?" Mothers always seemed to mention boys when a girl talked about someone liking or noticing them.

"Well, everyone did. They seemed to talk to me more.

It was just a class spelling bee anyway. Not like a real big deal, but it made me feel good."

"Well, there ya go," she said, taking another bite.

I had to write down what I was feeling about the topic so I took my sandwich back to my room. Mom didn't care and it actually made me feel better talking to her.

I started writing, but ended up with a different idea. One that had more meaning. My topic changed to how it felt to be blindsided by a crush. I wouldn't use Brad's name which would be a wise choice. I kept on writing, going over the word limit which was something I never did. Normally, I had to scrounge for words. The time passed so fast, I didn't even realize the sun was going down.

The paper also took my mind off of trying to see Officer Avalos the next day. I thought of going after school. Maybe asking Dad for the car to meet Tami somewhere. I did my best to put it out of my mind until I was on my way to school.

Chapter 25

I didn't hear from you yesterday," Tami told me on the bus. She was eating a small bag of nacho chips. "Were you, like, sleeping all day or what?"

"No, studying for this stupid science quiz," I told her. I wasn't up to talking about the paper with her. The strong odor of cheese was almost unbearable that early in the morning. I noticed it was a cheap brand.

"You actually studied?" She threw her head back and laughed. Her bouncy curls flew over the back of the seat.

"So?" I said. "I might as well try."

"Michelle, you are so, like, well nurtured or something."

"Whatever," I said. "I don't wanna have to take this class again. That's why." Little did she know I wasn't so well nurtured with what I was going to be telling the police. I kept telling myself not to let it out. I didn't want her going with me and then risk having the news all over town. Mom would find out and then she would really hit the roof. I wasn't ready to chance trying out my request that Mother should calm down and listen to me first, before tearing into me. I just hoped that if I used Tami as an alibi to get out of the house, Mom or Dad didn't see her somewhere when she was supposed to be with me. I planned on telling them we were going to study or to Wrap N Roll and Tami couldn't get access to either of her parents' cars.

"Have you heard anything yet?" she asked. "About, you know?"

"Tami, it's only been two days!"

"Chill out, I just asked!"

"The news will be out before I even find out myself probably. I'm surprised it hasn't been on the news."

"Nobody's contacted them yet."

"How do you know that?" What did she do, call them and ask? I thought.

"Well, doesn't somebody have to, like, contact the news to tell them about it? They just don't automatically know."

"Okay, Miss News Expert," I said. "I wonder if anyone else at school has heard."

"Who knows," she said, almost like she was disgusted. "I'm not telling anyone and Brad never really talks to anyone so I don't see them knowing about it yet."

"Let's hope they don't," I said. "I'm not up to the stares or questions I will be getting." All of a sudden, I halfway understood my mother's feelings.

"Uh-huh," she said, chewing. Then for some reason she uttered, "Wonder how Sean is."

"Why are you bringing him up?" I asked. I was really

getting tired of hearing about him.

"Well, just wondering if he, like, skipped town or something."

"No, not with all his property around here," I said, joking.

"Very funny," she said, continuing to eat her nacho breakfast.

Classes went surprisingly well. People didn't seem like they knew anything different about me. Like Tami said, the press must not have heard.

Brad didn't even say much to me except the same question Tami asked. I told him I would tell him whenever we found out anything new. We were all keeping it quiet which was a surprise with Tami's mouth. Sometimes she could get to yapping about stuff to the wrong person or someone could overhear her voice which seemed to carry through the halls of Giles High.

I felt good after science class, since I did well on the quiz. I was feeling great, like a breath of fresh air, until I was almost out of the building. That was when Tiffany approached me.

"Well, if it isn't the grave digger," she said. Her two best buddies laughed as if it were a funny remark.

I kept walking to the bus without even turning to look at her. It took all I had not to slap her a good one, but I didn't want to miss the bus by wasting my time talking to someone who refused to grow up.

"Why don't you take your pooch to the cemetery?" she yelled, her voice fading into existence as I kept on walking.

"Hey, your face is red!" Tami said when I arrived at our seat. "What happened?"

"That Tiffany bitch, that's what!" I said, sitting.

"Did you, like, mess up her hair again?" She laughed.

"No!" I said angered.

"Calm down! What happened?"

"I just ignored her. Calling me a grave digger."

"What? That's the best she could come up with?"

I took a deep breath to calm my nerves.

"Don't worry about her."

"I'm not," I said, my eyes resting on the back of a freshman's head. His hair was as white as Tiffany's, in the style of a bowl cut.

"She's just jealous she isn't the talk of the town."

"That's just it!" I looked over at her. "How did she hear about it?"

Tami then stood up to the window and opened it. "Hey!" she yelled. "Tiffany, did your mom sleep with the neighbor again? I heard she had him on top of the kitchen table!"

Tiffany was instantly angered as she scrunched up her face. It was almost as if she was going to start breathing fire. Instead, she stomped off quickly in another direction.

That got me laughing.

"People must be talking," Tami said.

"Wonder if the news knows about it yet."

"I dunno. I mean, it's, like, all over with now."

"No, it isn't!"

"The finding of the body is," she said. "Just because they haven't confirmed it's Luanne yet."

The bus started taking off. I bit my tongue, telling myself not to tell her what I was planning. If there was no way to get out of the house, I'd call and tell her to come pick me up, but if I could get use of the car, I was going for it on my own.

I arrived home and found Dad on the couch, watching Court TV. Buster relaxed next to him, his chin resting on Dad's leg.

"Hey, how was school?" he asked.

"Not bad. I did great on my science quiz."

"That's a surprise," he said joking.

"Very funny!" I said, sarcastically.

I went to my room and put my books down with Buster at my heels. I bent down and rubbed his ears. I hadn't walked him in a while so I promised him I would do it later. But, first things first.

Chapter 26

My heart was pounding, thinking of how to ask Dad for his car. This was something I never did, since I hadn't had my license very long. The police station was in Marian, about fifteen miles away. I had never driven on the highway yet, but I knew how to get to the station. Dad didn't pay attention to his miles on his car, especially since we had access to it while he was gone. It had to be done now. I couldn't wait any longer as I kissed Buster on his nose and picked up my accounting book before heading back down the hall.

"Um, Dad," I said, approaching the couch.

"Uh huh?" he asked, his eyes still on the television.

"Tami asked if I could go with her to Wrap N Roll, but she can't use her parents car since they're not home." I was glad he wasn't looking at me, since I was a terrible liar. "Could I take yours?"

He turned his head and looked at me. "Yeah, that's okay. I'm not going anywhere. Your mom might be making dinner later though."

"Oh, I know. I usually just get a snack size wrap. She just wants to go over our accounting homework and she didn't eat much at lunch time." I stopped talking, trying not to overdo it.

"Okay, the keys are on the hook." He went back to watching television.

I was relieved as I reached for the keys.

"Oh," he said, turning back to me. "Here." He handed me a ten dollar bill from his wallet. "Could you bring me back a turkey and swiss?"

I almost panicked. "What about Mom's dinner? We might be a while with this accounting. Tami is always having trouble."

"Oh yeah, you're right. We have leftovers anyway."

"Thanks Dad." I said, heading out the door.

I drove as fast as the speed limit would allow, heading to the highway. I hoped Mother wasn't getting off work early. She recently started getting weekends off since she had been at the shop as long as the owner had.

When I made it to the highway, I breathed a great sigh of relief. Tension subsided and I was able to drive much better.

There were many cars parked in the lot, so I had to park on the street. As I turned off the engine, I just happened to look up toward the building. My mouth dropped at what I saw. My heart started pounding. It couldn't be, could it? Her hair was stringy and hanging in her face, but it was the same auburn color. Fiery when the sunshine hit it. It was

KELLI SUE LANDON

Katie. It had to be. She was walking across the lot with some older man. He wore a ragged tee shirt and had wild sandy colored hair that was in great need of a combing. He was tanned and his arms appeared dirty along with his jeans and black work boots. He was wiping sweat off his forehead with his arm.

I almost went to grab my phone to call Tami, but then she would ask why I went to the police without her. They got into a silver mini van and pulled out of the lot. I was going to drive in to get their space so I started the car. Instinct took me another way. Without thinking, I followed the van.

I didn't think about how far I'd go in Dad's car. I just kept on driving, staying back enough so they wouldn't suspect I was following them. If I lost the van, I'd probably never find Katie again. The police must have been questioning her about Luanne. I wondered if they told her it was Luanne's body buried in the yard or if she knew the killer was Sean. My heart pounded and my palms were sweating so I turned on the air.

"Katie," I said to myself, "where have you been?"

That was going to be my first question when I got to where she was going. I had many questions. Too many to get out in time to make it back to the police station, then home.

I didn't look at the clock in the car. I figured it was okay to lose track of time. I did that all the time when I studied so that's what I would tell Dad if he asked what took so long.

The car ride only lasted about fifteen minutes but seemed like an eternity. We didn't even go back to the highway. We ended up on the outside of Marian. On the other side of town, the mini van pulled into Brookview Estates. This was an upscale neighborhood with brick homes and cobblestone walkways. Some homes appeared to be built with stone. It entered my mind how someone, who looked like the driver of the van, could afford such a nice place in a neighborhood like this.

The van pulled into a circular driveway made of red brick. I pulled up in front of the home, which reminded me of a two story gingerbread house. It had a very homey feel with flower boxes under the windows and a big arch-way above the front porch. The roof was bungalow style. I didn't want to worry about backing out, and I wasn't sure how long I'd be there, so I stayed on the street.

They got out of the van as the man looked back at me. I hurried and shut off the engine. Getting out of my dad's car, I called "Hey Katie!" as I waved.

She turned. "Michelle?" Her face lit up as she started walking toward me, carrying an armful of books. "Michelle! Hey, what-"

The man stopped her. "Katie, in the house!" he demanded.

She reluctantly turned, walked up the steps which led to a big porch, and into the house.

"May I help you?" the man asked me.

I shook my head. I felt my face flush. "Um, no," I stammered. "I'm just a classmate of Katie's."

"Oh, you go to Crestline?" He put his hands on his hips.

I noticed with his posture and the way he carried himself, he was very athletic. He reminded me of someone who could have been a California surfer if his hair looked nicer.

"No, an old classmate," I said.

"Well, Katie is busy. Don't be bothering her. She has homework." Turning away from me, he wiped his arm across his forehead.

"I'm sorry," I said as sincerely as I could.

He walked away, up the porch, and looked back at me once before entering the house.

I was angry. I wanted so bad to go pound on the door. I wanted questions answered and I had waited far too long. I also wanted my book back. I didn't want to risk them calling the police on me disturbing the peace, so I let it go. I saw a curtain pull back on one of the upstairs windows, just below the right side of the roof. I couldn't see anyone but I wondered if it was Katie's room. I also wondered where Deedee was. I assumed she was with a different family.

I got back into Dad's car and wrote down the address. I also wrote down the code of my phone number on a piece of paper. Katie had my number and the easy way to remember it, but she never called me. She never had a cell phone that I knew of. My number spelled out MISS YOU on the phone key pad. I wrote down MISS YOU, KATIE and then I thought a moment before adding DO YOU STILL

HAVE MY BOOK I LENT YOU? I got out of the car and looked up at the window. I could see a little bit of a face and long hair. I held up the small piece of paper and put it in the mailbox. This was a gamble since it was against the law to open another person's mailbox, but I had no where else to put it. The mailbox was empty so someone must have gotten the mail or they didn't get any that day. A wave of a hand came from the window when I returned to the car.

I drove back to the police station, mortified over the way that man treated me. I knew upscale neighborhoods had the reputation of snobby residents, but I wasn't entirely sure it was true. I didn't deserve to be treated that way. Crestline or Giles High, what did it matter? So I wasn't an upscale snob, did that mean I couldn't talk to an old friend? I wanted to tear into him so bad. I didn't realize I was gripping the steering wheel so tight until I turned. I loosened my grip and felt the tension release.

I made it back to the police station, still fuming.

"Officer Avalos please!" I demanded at the counter.

"Hold your horses there, little Ms. Thang!" A young geeky officer told me. "He is very busy. What's your name?"

"Michelle Martin."

He squinted his eyes at me through thick framed glasses. "Oh, hold on. I will tell him you're here."

"Pencil neck," I said quietly, pacing the floor.

He turned back to look at me, but kept walking. He had a feminine way about him as he swayed his hips. A few seconds later, he returned.

"Well what do ya know?" he said. "He just now got a break."

I folded my arms. "Well, can I go in?"

"Sure, come on, I'll take you. Having a bad day? You are a sassy one!" he said, walking me back.

"Not too good," I said.

When we got to Officer Avalos's office, he told me to sit down across from him.

"Hello, Michelle," he said, twirling a pen in between his fingers. "Nice to see you."

"Yeah." I took a deep breath. "Katie just left?"

His eyes fixated on me. "Yeah, we found her. What did you want to see me about?"

"I know what the deal is."

"What deal?" he asked.

"Who the body is."

"Oh, you mean who the body belongs to," he corrected. "Well you are one up on the authorities then." He dropped the pen on his desk and leaned back in his chair. "Who so you think it is?"

"It's gotta be Luanne."

"And what makes you so sure?"

"Well, she was having an affair with Sean. He killed her in a crime of passion. Easy as that."

"Uh huh," he said, leaning forward onto his desk. "And you know this because?"

"It's obvious!" I was getting agitated at him looking at

me like he didn't believe me. "We all knew her reputation around town."

"That's here say."

"So? It's the truth!"

"Don't be getting all excited now!" He extended his hands as he talked. "And don't be talking about this all around town. This is how rumors get started."

I nodded. "Well, do you know who it is?"

"No. Nobody has been reported missing which makes it harder. But, I can tell you one thing."

"What's that?" I asked.

"The press is gonna be all over this soon. I'm expecting it any minute now. I guess I can tell you, even though I probably shouldn't." He paused.

"What is it?" I asked impatiently.

"The body belongs to a male, Michelle."

Chapter 27

A male?" I asked. "Did I hear that right?"
This was all wrong, I thought. How could that be? I was shocked. It was as if Officer Avalos was mistaken or pulling my leg.

"Yes, we know how to tell what sex the body is." He sounded as if he were joking.

"I don't believe it," I said, shaking my head.

"Well, do you want to see the body for yourself?"

I shook my head again. "No," I told him. "You don't know who it is?"

"Oh, believe me, we are doing everything we can to find out. That's why we are questioning everyone who knew the woman that lived in the house."

"Luanne?" I asked.

"Yes, Luanne. Your mother is also on the list."

Oh no, I thought. "Um, could you not tell her I was here?"

He didn't answer.

"Please?" I asked with a fake smile. "She won't like that

I came to you with this story of mine."

"Sure." He nodded. "I won't tell her if you promise not to spread any more stories around about this. You could have had the whole neighborhood in an uproar thinking Luanne was killed and buried in her backyard."

"Well someone was killed and buried. People are gonna wanna know who did it."

"Michelle, that's enough," he said sternly. "We can't answer questions especially when we don't know who the deceased person is. I just assure everyone that we will get who is responsible. There are no signs of a mass murderer out there. Now, I need to get back to work."

I got up slowly. "I'm sorry," I told him as I exited his office.

Walking to the car, I was still in shock. I got in and took my phone out of my purse. I had to call Tami. I was in the car alone so I had plenty of privacy.

"A man?" she asked when I told her.

"Yeah, I don't get it."

"Well, who the hell is it?"

"I dunno," I said. "Look, don't tell anyone I told you okay? The officer isn't happy that I thought it was Luanne. He doesn't like rumors."

"Well, nobody does!" she said matter of factly. "And why didn't you tell me you were up to this? I would have went with you!"

"Tami, there's more I gotta tell ya." I couldn't hold back any more about Katie. "Whatever you do, do not tell Brad."

"Okay," she said.

"I mean it!" I demanded. "Nobody can know this. Don't tell anyone or it may get back to him or my parents."

"Okay, Michelle!" she said. "What is it?"

"I found her."

"Who?" she asked. "Luanne? Where?"

"No, Katie! I saw her coming out of the police station and I followed her. She was with some man who was a jerk! He wouldn't even let me talk to her!"

"Oh my God! What did he look like?"

"Who cares?" I couldn't believe Tami was pulling this. She was so guy crazy, it was nuts.

"Michelle, I mean, did he look like her? Maybe it was her real dad."

I hadn't thought of that. "No, I didn't see a resemblance."

"Where was her mother? Was she, like, in the car too?"

"No, there wasn't anyone with them. Maybe she was at work. They live in Brookview Estates."

"Wow!" she said. "Did they have a pool?"

"I dunno Tami, I didn't go in the backyard!" I was appalled at her questions. "There's more serious stuff going on here than a pool!" Or even an autographed out of print book that my grandmother left me, I thought.

"What did you say?"

"Just that I was a classmate of hers and he asked if I went to Crestline too."

"Oh, now that's a fancy dancy school. Don't they, like,

wear uniforms or something?"

"Katie didn't have one on. Look, if Mom or Dad asks, I was with you today at Wrap N Roll studying."

She laughed. "Michelle! You crack me up!"

"This isn't funny!" I said. "I gave Katie the code to my phone number and put it in her mailbox."

"Okay, now that is against the law."

"Yeah, I know, but I had no other choice."

"What if her dad gets it? Did he see you?"

"I don't care," I said. "All it says is, miss you Katie and I asked about my book."

"Oh yeah, that book," she said as if she forgot. "I'm gonna be going there soon."

"Where?" My heart started racing for fear that she was going to show up at Katie's house.

"The police station. I guess they wanna question me too."

"Good luck," I told her.

"Yeah, but I don't have much to tell."

"That's good! I wish I didn't. Okay, I gotta go," I told her. "I wanna make it home before Mom."

"Have fun with that!" she said. "I will call you later!"

I hurried home as fast as I could. I was in luck. Mom wasn't home when I got there.

"That didn't take long!" Dad said when I walked into the house. He was sitting in the exact same place he was when I left.

"Didn't you eat?" I asked him, changing the subject.

"Oh, I was going to, but I got into this court show."

I promised Buster a walk so I grabbed his leash and did my best to snap it on him while he jumped repeatedly with excitement.

We walked the opposite way, away from Katie's old house. I had to admit, It wasn't exciting. Many houses down this way were owned by old people who stayed inside all day. Mr. Nichols was old, but at least he was entertaining.

I felt better after the walk and spending time with Buster made me forget everything for a little while. When we arrived home, I hung up Buster's leash and went straight to my room.

The dead guy crossed my mind. Who could it be? I wondered if Katie got the note I left. I hoped she would call. With the strict father she now had, I didn't think she would have a cell phone. She'd have to sneak a call to me.

When my phone rang just after dinner, I ran to my room and snatched it off my dresser, thinking it was Katie. To my disappointment, it was Tami. I forgot she said she was going to call.

"Yes?" I said, answering.

"Well, aren't you cheery?" she said sarcastically. "Michelle, that cop is to die for!"

Oh no, I thought. She's hot for Officer Avalos. "Yeah, he's okay."

"Okay? Are you blind or what?" She had the same excitement in her voice as she did when she talked about Sean.

"You are not going to ask him out, are you?" I asked. "That is, unless you haven't already."

"Michelle, he is like, too old! Plus he's married."

"That never stopped you before!" I said.

"You don't mess with a married cop! They are married to strong women who don't take no shit!"

"Whatever!" I had no idea where she heard this tidbit of information. "Well, what happened?"

"Nothing, just said we went to look at the house and that was that."

"Did you tell him you were hot for Sean?" I asked, jokingly.

"No! I wouldn't tell the cops that! That's none of their business!"

I got a laugh out of her remark.

The conversation was pretty short since we didn't have much more to talk about. I told her I would see her tomorrow on the bus and we ended the call.

The rest of the night went pretty well until the ten o'clock news started.

I was getting ready for bed when I heard Mom announce, "Here it is!"

I came out of my room and stood in the hallway, watching the television from there. It showed the rental house behind a blonde newscaster with dark purple lipstick and big teeth.

"The quiet town of Giles is rocked by a grisly discovery," the woman announced. "A body was found buried in the backyard of a house here on Redwood Drive. The body is yet to be identified, but is that of a male, possibly in his fifties. It appears that he died by blunt force trauma and a knife wound. No other information is available at this time, but police are searching for Luanne White, the woman who rented the house. Anyone with any information as to where Ms. White is, please contact your local police department."

She ended with the phone number that appeared on the screen.

"A male!" Mom said out loud. "Who would that be? Someone she was screwing?"

"Come on Nancy!" Dad said, turning down the television. "You don't know if she had anything to do with it."

"You know how she was, Bill! You even had a hard on for her and don't you deny it!" Mom yelled.

I took it they didn't realize I was standing in the hallway.

"What are you talking about?" Dad said, standing from the sofa. "I never looked at that woman twice!"

"You didn't have to!" Mom's voice was getting louder. "The whole town knew you only had to look once at that piece of ass!"

"Where are these accusations coming from?" He put his hands on his hips. "You've never said anything about this before!"

"No, I haven't, but it's been all over town that she's slept with every Tom, Dick and Harry who lives here!"

"Yeah, rumors from your local beauty shop gossip!"

Mom walked away, into the kitchen while ranting. "You sure liked her in her cut off shorts, didn't you?"

I thought of Mr. Nichols talking about that. He sure liked her.

"Just because she's all out there, doesn't mean I liked her! She-" he stopped when he noticed me. "Sorry, hon. We keeping you up?"

Mom peeked around the corner from the kitchen. "Go to bed!" she demanded.

I felt bad about her accusing Dad like that. I walked slowly to my room with Buster following me as fast as his little legs would allow. I could tell he was afraid of Mom's tone. I never heard any more arguing that night as I laid in bed crying while Buster slept alongside me.

Why did I have to go in that yard? I thought. I knew I did a good thing, but it caused such a turmoil in my family and neighborhood. I only hoped Dad didn't hurry on to his next job on the road. I didn't want to be here alone with Mom in this state.

Chapter 28

The next day on the bus I told Tami all about the news and fight between Mom and Dad.

"Oh man," she said. "Are they gonna, like, get divorced now?"

I shrugged, looking down at my lap. "I dunno, but I bet Dad can't wait to get back on the road. He was sleeping on the couch when I left."

I noticed it being real quiet on the bus while we talked. I realized everyone must have seen the news. My name wasn't mentioned but I was sure they all knew I was the one who found the body.

"I went to bed early," Tami said. "Missed the news."

I shushed her. "People are listening," I whispered.

"Oh!" she said loudly "So, did you hear about Tiffany? Her mom got caught with the pizza delivery boy outside! They were getting it on in the driveway! She must not have had the money to pay the guy!"

I let out a big laugh, making my eyes water. I was laughing to hard, I felt a gag in my throat. We were surrounded with people snickering. Tami always knew how to bring me out of my slump.

When we walked into the building, I noticed Krystal in her all black getup with her black hair sprouting purple streaks. She smiled at me. What shocked me even more than her smiling, was her perfectly straight white teeth. They almost looked fake.

"Hey, cool!" was all she said to me as I passed.

"Cool hair!" I told her. I didn't think she went to Cutting Edge since they didn't do non-human colors.

"How are you?" Brad asked when I passed him in the hall.

"Good," I said, stopping. I didn't feel like talking to him. I always worried that he was going to bombard me with questions. "Why?"

"Just wondering. The news is out."

"Yeah, but my name wasn't mentioned. Somehow everyone knows I was the one who found the body." Nobody could hear me over the loud chatter and lockers slamming shut around us.

"They heard about it from the start," he explained. "They just didn't know if it was true about the body being in the backyard, but now they do."

"Oh really?" I said sarcastically.

"Yeah, really," he said, mimicking me. "You act like you don't believe me."

"No, I do," I said. "I just didn't know you talked to everyone in the school."

"Michelle, I hear things. What's up with you?"

"Nothing. I just gotta get to class."

"Okay, see ya," he said turning away.

"Thanks for telling me about it," I called after him.

He didn't turn back.

I felt a tad bad about not telling him I saw Katie. I hoped Tami didn't let him know. I was afraid he would go ballistic and demand to know her address.

Everything was going great until lunch time. Tami and I were at our regular table enjoying our hot dogs and side of buttered corn when Tiffany appeared with her two friends. She had one hand on her hip as she twisted her hair with the other. Her makeup was done in pink. Pink blush, pink lipstick and pink eye shadow complete with glitter.

"Hmmm." she said.

"Well, if it isn't frick and frack standing behind the queen." Tami said before taking a bite of her hot dog.

"You may wanna ease up on that eating," Tiffany told her. "Getting a little cushiony in the behind."

"Why are you checking out my ass?" Tami said with a mouthful.

I snickered.

"Oh, ha ha, Miss Michelle," she said to me. "Have you gone digging for any more corpses? I hear you been hanging out with Krystal."

At that time, Krystal shot up from her table, across the room.

I took it Tiffany didn't know Krystal could hear that far

away. She had the deer-in-the-headlights look.

"Um," Tiffany said, turning halfway to catch a glimpse of Krystal. "Well, have you?"

I just shook my head, trying my best not to laugh.

"We think you did this all for the attention," she said. "Now you seem to be the talk of the school."

I found this ironic since I hated attention. I shrugged. "So? Jealous?"

"Tiff is never jealous of anything. Your mom sure seems to be though."

That did it. I grabbed my open milk carton and threw it at her. Milk sloshed all over Tiffany. It dripped down from her hair onto her pink fuzzy blouse.

It happened so fast, I didn't even realize I had done it until the three of them started brushing themselves off and running away to the bathroom. Tiffany was yelling about her makeup.

Everyone clapped but I got sent to the office by Mr. Haywood, our monitor. I got off with a slap on the wrist since I had been through so much turmoil lately, not to mention I had many witnesses who saw Tiffany approach me first.

"Boy," Tami said the next time she saw me, "you got her a good one!"

"Yeah, but how did she hear about Mom and Dad fighting?"

"Maybe someone on the bus overheard you this morning," she said. "Or it could be that your mom has been, like, complaining about your dad and Luanne at the shop."

"Well, she had no right talking about my mom like that! That is none of her business!" I said, walking into accounting class.

"Okay Michelle, you are getting all red."

"I don't care!" I said louder, dropping my books on my desk. "She is a little bitch!"

At that time, Ms. Runyon came into the classroom.

"Okay, enough insults for today Michelle," she said nonchalantly.

I looked around the room and everyone got quiet. They all stared straight ahead at the board, except for Brad. He had a big smile on his face, laughing to himself.

Tami slid over a note on my desk.

It read, Did she call yet?

I shook my head at her. I figured she was talking about Katie. We weren't allowed to have our phones in class, but I checked mine at my locker when I had time to stop between classes. I hoped Brad didn't see the note, but I would just tell him we were talking about my mom if he asked.

Chapter 29

That night around seven o'clock, I was doing my homework when I got a text from Brad. He asked if I could talk. I answered him, saying that I could. A couple seconds later, my phone rang.

"Hello?" I answered, wondering what he wanted.

"I went to see her," he said.

Oh no. Somehow he found out where Katie was, I thought.

"Katie?" I asked.

"No! Katie? Why would you say that?"

"I dunno," I said, feeling like an idiot. I should have kept my mouth shut. "I just didn't know who you meant."

"Betty. Duh!"

I laughed nervously. "Oh. What happened?"

"I demanded to know what was going on and wasn't taking no for an answer."

"And?" I was getting concerned at what he found out. I hoped he didn't threaten the woman.

"She said someone has taken Katie into their home and

are lovely parents, but she wouldn't say where."

Yeah, lovely, I thought. "What about Luanne or Deedee? Did she say anything about them?"

"Just that Deedee was fostered out somewhere else before Katie was. I told her I wanted to know why she never said goodbye. I put on a big sad performance and she took the bait."

"Well, why?" I wanted him to get to the point.

"She said Luanne was too promiscuous. She wasn't fit to raise the kids so she took them away from her. Sean, the prick, reported back to Betty about Luanne coming onto him, trying to get him into bed."

"That's it?" I didn't mean to show the disappointment in my voice.

"Well, sorry it's not some big, big news you were wanting."

"Sorry, Brad. I didn't know the girls were taken away from her."

"Yeah and you know what else? Betty said Luanne's past was almost non-existent."

"What do you mean?"

"They couldn't find anything out about her before she moved here. You have to have some sort of background information in order to legally adopt someone."

"Like what?"

"I dunno. I guess they do a background check, so I would think she would have had to have proof of where she lived before and any employment she had. They don't give kids to just anyone, unless you pay big bucks. They let her foster them because they were overloaded on kids and needed to find places for them temporarily."

"Oh man, so Luanne never had a chance of adopting them then."

"Unless she had money stashed away. I also bet Sean lied," he said, after a short pause.

"Why do you say that?"

"Is there really proof that Luanne slept around?"

I paused, thinking.

"Come on Michelle, name off one guy she had an affair with that you know of."

"Well, nobody, I guess."

"Right."

"But that doesn't mean it didn't happen. I thought it was Sean who she was sleeping with."

"Those two are way mismatched."

Yeah, but Tami liked him too, I thought. On the other hand, I could see someone like Sean making up the story that Luanne wanted him to make himself look like the town stud. He struck me as that type with the way he was talking to Tami. Then it dawned on me. I wondered if that's why Tami took interest in him in the first place.

"I don't trust that guy," he said. "I feel like paying him a little visit too."

"You could get in trouble," I told him.

"What trouble?"

"Well, Sean could call the police on you for showing up,

thinking you are there to fight."

He laughed. "Yeah, and he couldn't touch me since I'm a minor. Hey, thanks for the idea!"

"Brad!" I was freaking out and couldn't tell if he was kidding. "Don't be doing anything crazy!"

"I won't," he said. "I'm just joshing you. Oh, and he is the one who took the girls back to Betty that day Luanne left. Supposedly she took off and left the girls home that morning when Betty informed her that they are going to be coming back into child services, or whatever you call it."

"That's weird," I said. "Well, that explains Mr. Nichols's story about them leaving in an SUV."

"Yeah, but it still sounds fishy. That's why I wanna ask him a thing or two."

"Are you going to his place?"

"I might. Wanna tag along?"

I thought about it for a minute. I could tell Mom we were going to get ice cream. I'd been studying all evening, only stopping for a snack. She didn't cook anything since she and Dad weren't talking.

"Okay, lemme ask my mom and I'll text you back."

Mom and Dad didn't care either way if I went with Brad, Tami, or by myself. They were both in their own worlds, one watching television and the other reading a book while guzzling a glass of wine. I overheard Mom say earlier that she had to go to the station for questioning, but she never mentioned how it went.

The perfect family, I thought as I slipped into my sneakers

and took a brush through my hair. Buster started jumping up and down, thinking I was getting ready for a walk.

"Not tonight, Bud," I told him, patting his head.

It was then that I realized, lying was getting easier.

Chapter 30

I hoped the trip to Sean's wouldn't take long. Who knew if he would even talk to us.

"I got his address from the phone book," Brad said, driving.

"Yeah, Tami's been there too."

"Oh, that's a surprise," he said sarcastically.

We pulled up and saw a light on in the living room.

"Well, they're home!" he said, cutting the engine.

Brad stomped up the driveway and banged on the door with the side of his fist.

I hurried to keep up with him. "Don't you think that's a little loud?"

"Just want them to hear me."

A dog barked ferociously in the dark next door. I was hoping he couldn't jump the fence.

"They're not that far away," I said, pointing to the window. I could see a woman coming to the door.

"Yes?" she asked, opening the door as a glowing orange porch light came on. She was a small, mousy looking thing.

Her eyes were red and puffy and she was wearing an old ladies nightgown that buttoned up to her neck. Her hair was
a long frizzed out mess. I thought mine was hard to get a
comb through, but this was horrific.

"Is Sean here?" Brad said. "I got some questions for him."

The woman screamed, slammed the door and locked it.
"Go away!" she yelled.

"Oh, I'm sorry. I didn't mean to scare you," Brad said.
"I'm just looking for Luanne."

My mouth dropped. I lightly slapped Brad's shoulder.

"What?" He whispered.

We heard the lock click and she opened the door just
enough so we could see her face.

"That slut who banged my husband?" she asked in a
harsh tone. Her glare was like ice, slicing through us.

My mouth dropped again. I did not expect those words
to come out of this frail looking woman. She even thought
Luanne was sleeping with him. I looked at Brad who just
stood there frozen, his eyes fixating on her.

"Is that who you are looking for?" she asked. "The police have been asking about her too."

"She never slept with Sean, did she?" Brad asked.

"I'd bet my life savings on it."

We all shared a small silence except for the dog barking repeatedly next door. The woman finally spoke again.
"SHUT UP ARCHIE!" She screamed.

The dog whined as if he were upset that he had to stop
barking.

"It's her fault he's dead," she said.

"Who?" Brad asked.

At first, I thought she was talking about the dead body in the backyard.

"Sean!" she said, almost crying. "Hit and run. Didn't you hear?" She started sobbing loudly and slammed the door.

We just stood here, gawking at each other as mosquitos flew between us.

"No way," I said, waving the bugs away. "This is weird."

"Maybe it was just an accident," he said. "Maybe they are just thinking it was a hit and run."

"I dunno," I said. "This is crazy, but I wonder if Luanne is in town."

"You think she hit him?"

"Well, we have a dead body in her backyard and now her married lover is dead. Sounds like Luanne would be the one to suspect. His wife even thinks so."

"I just can't see her sleeping with him."

"Will you get off of that!" I was appalled that he was still thinking of those two having an affair when other matters were at stake.

"GET OFF MY PORCH!" We heard the woman yell from inside.

We got back into the car and started on our way home.

"We will have to sleep on this," he said.

My stomach did a flip flop, thinking of us sleeping on

something like we were a couple. Stop it, I thought. Brad and I were never going to happen.

We talked the whole way home about why Luanne would do something like this. We didn't think she had it in her, but she was the only person I could think of who had some sort of motive to kill Sean. Maybe it was revenge for telling Betty about her private life, but I wouldn't think that would be something someone would kill for. The only other person I could think of was one of his renters. He was wanting money from the one that Tami saw through the window. But why would someone kill someone over rent money? My mind was racing as Brad dropped me off home.

"Thanks for going along," he said, looking at me sweetly.

"Sure, no problem." I kept my guard up, not giving in to his smile.

As I walked to the front door, I felt a stab of guilt from keeping the news of Katie quiet. Entering the house, I was shocked to learn that Mom and Dad were in the bedroom, earlier than usual. Apparently, they had made up.

Chapter 31

A hit and run?" Tami asked wide eyed. "Are you sure?"
"That's what she said," I told her.

The school bus was noisy that day so we spoke in our normal tones. Sometimes I had to talk quite loud so Tami could hear me.

"Oh my God! How did this happen?" she asked.

"I guess someone hit him with a car. I turned on the news for a few minutes last night, but nothing was said. I think it had just happened. His wife was crying really bad."

"Did she say anything else?" She tore open a package of cheese crackers sandwiched with peanut butter.

"No," I said, noticing the agitated look she was giving me. I couldn't tell if it was from Sean or hunger. "I'm sorry. I didn't know how to tell you and I wanted to break the news in person."

"Oh no, that's all right." She shrugged it off like it was no big deal. "I guess he had it coming, especially since he was, like, doing Luanne."

"Everybody thinks that," I told her.

"Don't you? His wife does, since she blurted out that Luanne was a slut. I'll bet he was sniffing around her house."

There was a short pause as the chatter and laughing continued all around us. Then she spoke again, holding a cracker. "Hey, maybe I should go talk to her."

I was shocked at her suggestion. I could tell this was bothering her, but there was no way I would go with her to check this out. We had been fishing around enough and I wasn't up for it.

"No way!" I said flat out. "Do not do this, Tami!"

"Calm down. I was kidding," she said, popping the cracker in her mouth.

"You better be!" I took a deep breath. This was a relief, but I was hoping she really was kidding and not just saying it to shut me up.

After swallowing, she said, "The whole thing just makes me mad. You know, about him and Luanne."

"Why? You are upset over him doing something before he even knew you? That makes no sense! I can see his wife being upset, but you?"

"Well, no I'm not upset. Just feel like I failed or something."

"Failed at what?" I didn't understand her thinking at all.

"Failed to get him, like, interested in me."

"Tami, he was married! His wife was probably home a

lot and he couldn't get away. You need to let it go!"

"I have," she said. "It just makes me wonder, that's all."

"Well, the wondering should be over now. He's gone."

She put her head down. "It is kind of sad. I mean, what did he do to ask for this? Besides mess around on his wife?"

I wasn't sure who killed Sean or why. If it was Luanne, the motive was clear, but who else would have done it? It dawned on me that it could have been his wife, but she was too broken up. I put that thought out of my mind the second it came. If anyone else would have seen her besides me and Brad, they would rule her out too. I actually felt sorry for her.

I went to the bathroom after my English Composition class. While I was in one of the stalls, a couple of girls came in rambling. I didn't recognize the voices, but I smelled cigarette smoke.

"Well, I heard she was terrible to those girls," one girl said. "She would parade them out on dates with her and the married men."

Oh, now it was men instead of man, I thought, shaking my head.

"Really? Who told you that?"

"Nobody, I just know. I saw her when I went into the store and she was always talking to the manager guy. I'm sure she had him too."

I quietly zipped up my jeans. In a split second, I flushed the toilet just before swinging the stall door open. The girls jumped and threw their cigarettes in the sink and took off.

"I thought you looked under the stall!" one of them said as they scurried out.

They were two freshmen. It was my recollection that they thought they were being sneaky by smoking out in the open and didn't know I was in the bathroom.

By the end of the day, I heard another story. Two guys were whispering in science class that they thought Luanne was still in town.

"She's probably watching and waiting, decked out in camouflage," one guy said.

"Oh yeah, she is probably dressed in a camouflage bikini with long thigh high boots! Body paint would be hot too!"

They snickered as Mr. Beaverton glared over his eyeglasses at them.

"Something to share with the class boys?" he asked.

One guy cleared his throat and said no.

It sickened me the way people just drew their own conclusions to what happened. I even speculated Sean sleeping with her, but didn't go to extremes by adding camouflage to the list. Guys made everything sexual and it made me resent them. It was sad with Luanne getting a reputation when she wasn't even in the neighborhood anymore. At least I didn't think she was.

On the bus ride home, my phone rang. I looked at it, but didn't recognize the number.

"Who is this?" I said, looking at my phone.

"What is it?" Tami asked, drinking a grape soda.

A thought occurred to me that it could be Katie. I went ahead and hit the button to answer. "Hello."

"Michelle?" It was Katie. "Is this Michelle?"

"Yes!" I said with excitement, looking over at Tami. "Katie?"

Tami's eyes stopped dead in their sockets.

"Look, I don't have much time. I'm sneaking this call from the school office. School's out and the secretary left for a minute. I want you to meet me tomorrow."

"What?" I asked, shocked that she demanded I meet with her just out of the blue. "Where?"

"I can't get away by myself. It's gonna have to be here, at Crestline. I go to lunch at eleven-thirty. Meet me in back by the tennis courts. I'm sorry about everything, but I gotta go. My dad is waiting for me outside. Oh, and don't tell anyone." Click.

I sat there, staring into space.

"What?" Tami asked.

I hung up my phone. "Um, Katie wants me to meet her at her school tomorrow when she goes to lunch. How am I gonna manage this one?" I knew she didn't want me to tell anyone, but I didn't get why. I wasn't going to keep this from Tami when she was right there next to me.

She shrugged. "If it was me, I'd skip class." She took a drink of her soda, changing her lips to a purple hue. "I'll skip with you if you want."

"No," I told her. "She said not to tell anyone."

"Why? Is it because of the dead body?" she chuckled.

"I dunno," I said thinking. "How am I even supposed to get there? I don't drive to school."

"Take the bus. What I would do is tell them you aren't feeling well, wait outside for your mom to pick you up, then like, walk to the bus stop. They go directly into town. I mean, you know where the school is, so even if the bus doesn't go right by it, you can, like, walk a little. I think it stops there between ten-thirty and eleven for people who wanna go to lunch in town."

"I should have asked her where my book was, but she didn't give me a chance."

"Call back," she said.

"No, it was the school's number."

"Oh. Well, just take money for the bus if you plan on going. I'd also, like, forge a note just in case."

"A note for what?"

Tami was always one to forge her parents signature when they sent bad grade reports home. She did that all through grade school and never got caught.

"In case the person driving the bus asks why you aren't with a parent. You could say you were, like, going to the doctor. There's gotta be a doctor's office somewhere over by there."

"I could say I have a job during school hours. Other people get to leave for that."

"That's for seniors," Tami said. "Oh, you could say you are seventeen, I guess. It's only one year off."

I thought about what she said. I still had money that Dad gave me for my phantom trip to Wrap N Roll the other day when I followed Katie. It seemed like it could work. Only if I didn't get caught.

Later that evening, the scent of tomato sauce and garlic flowed in under my bedroom door. I was in my room most of the night, thinking about how to leave school and get to Katie without getting caught. I stressed out way too easy. I did get enough courage to write a note saying I had a doctor's appointment if I needed it.

I headed out of my room toward the smell of supper. Mom and Dad were standing side by side at the stove, cooking. Buster was at their feet, panting while waiting for something to be dropped.

"Oh!" Mom jumped when Dad smacked her behind.

I cleared my throat and took a seat at the table.

"Hey!" Dad turned to me holding a wooden spoon colored red from marinara sauce. "What brings you out of hibernation?"

"I was just studying." I lied. I was really lying on my bed, staring at the ceiling. "What's for dinner?"

"Spaghetti with sausage," Dad said.

"Mmmmm," Mom said, taking a taste of it. "It's wonderful!"

"I'm gonna be leaving again on Friday," he told me.

"Oh," I said with disappointment. "For how long?"

"Just a few days. I should be coming home Monday."

I was happy about the short trip, but hated to think about being home with Mother all weekend.

"Sorry," he said, going back to the stove. He must have read my mind.

"I'll miss his cooking for the weekend," Mom said without turning.

I wasn't about to ask her how it went at the police station. I didn't want to bring her out of her good mood.

We had a good dinner that night. The hot crusty garlic bread made it complete. I often wished I could have a glass of Mom's red wine with dinner, but I didn't dare ask. The conversation switched back and forth from school to their jobs, minus the gossip at Cutting Edge. I savored this moment. It was going to be one of my good memories to think about when things got tough. I had a feeling there were going to be more tough days ahead.

Chapter 32

Tami asked me the next morning if I was going to cut class.

"I dunno," I said quietly, looking around the bus. "I'm nervous."

"Why?" she asked. "I'll go with you if you want."

"No Tami, that would be too suspicious. You and me both cutting class? How would they believe I was sick?"

"This would be better if I had my mom or dad's car," she said.

I wished she could take me. I at least had to get that book back so I was hoping Katie would have it with her.

We talked quietly for the remainder of the ride to school.

"Have you heard anything else?" Brad asked me as I headed toward my locker.

"No, you?"

He shook his head. "No, but they talked about Sean on the news last night."

"They did?" I stopped dead in my tracks. I forgot about watching the news. I didn't think Mom and Dad had it on since they went to bed early.

"Yeah, just said they need any information from anyone who saw it."

"I take it nobody did."

"It happened in the middle of the day right in the neighborhood."

"By his house?" I asked.

"Just a few blocks down," Brad said.

"Oh man." I continued on my way as he followed.

"Yeah, people are worried about a killer running around. After the body being buried in the yard and now this. It does make you wonder, ya know?"

I nodded, turning the dial on my locker. "Yeah, it does. If you find out anything else, let me know, okay?"

"What's wrong?" he asked. "You look worried."

I shook my head. "No, just tired."

After my second class, I headed for the office, holding my stomach. It was a little early, but I wanted to do this between classes so I wouldn't have to tell a teacher about it and put on a horrible acting performance.

"Hey, Michelle," Olivia, the secretary, greeted. "What's wrong? You don't look so good."

"I called my dad to come and get me. I'm not feeling well." I did my best to make my voice sound weak. I was tired anyway so it wasn't hard.

"You wanna lie down in the back?"

"He won't be long," I told her. "I just wanted to let you know."

"Okay," she said. "If he is late or can't come to get you, come back and lie down. We don't need an epidemic going around the school."

I nodded as I left the office and shuffled out the front doors of the school. I sped up as I got closer to the bus stop. I walked three blocks and around the corner to where the bus stop was. I sat on the bench and waited. The time seemed to drag. Tami said the bus usually stopped around this time so I was hoping she was right. What if she is mistaken? I thought. I started to worry until I saw the bus appear a few minutes later.

"Finally," I said out loud.

The driver never asked who I was or why I was out of school when I paid the bus fare. I was surprised. Everyone seemed to be oblivious to a teenager on a bus by herself. I sat down quickly in the first seat I found.

There were two women seated across from me dressed in black, carrying brief cases like they were on a job. They were whispering to each other and checking their cell phones. There was a heavy set older man with wrinkled clothing sitting behind me. I could actually hear him breathing. It was getting on my nerves but I paid more attention to the area outside my window, hoping nobody saw me.

Would this guy stop his loud breathing? I thought. Was he watching the back of my head, wanting to know why a young girl would be on a city bus?

With the bus stops on the way, picking up a few more business looking people, it took about a good half an hour to get to the vicinity of Marian. I didn't see the school any-where, but I knew about where I was. We would always pass by the area when I went with Tami to the mall or out to eat. The Pizzeria wasn't far, but it was in the opposite direction.

I walked for about fifteen minutes, going slow since I was a little early. My backpack was getting heavy. I wasn't used to walking that far with my books.

The fresh air helped calm me down a little. I was para-noid that someone I knew might pass by. I walked by a gas station where an old man who looked like Mr. Nichols was pumping gas. I didn't look at him very long in case it happened to be him. A woman walking a golden retriever passed me. The dog made me think of Buster. He was probably bored, sleeping at home, wondering if I was ever going to walk him again. I wanted so much to bend down and pet the golden retriever, but I put it out of my mind. I had to focus on getting to the school. I wondered if Katie would be there, waiting for me.

I ended up arriving just about on time. I walked around the back of Crestline High School. The area was huge, complete with two tennis courts and a race track. I didn't see a football field but a big baseball diamond was on the other side, further away from the school grounds. As I waited by the tennis courts, I let my eyes wander the school yard. It was peaceful as the breeze blew lightly through the trees. There were houses across the street with immaculate backyards. Every one had different colored flowers growing along the fences. The swings from the swing sets swayed in the breeze.

Just then the back door opened abruptly.

"Hey!" said Katie walking down the steps to meet me. She hugged me tightly. "How have you been?" She had a wide smile and was carrying a white plastic sack. Her hair was neatly combed back from her forehead which made her look so much better than when I saw her last. Her cheeks were dotted lightly with freckles.

"Fine," I answered. "But things are not fine back home. Where have you been? Why didn't you say goodbye before going to Florida?"

She backed away and looked around the school grounds. "I have your book," she said, handing me the sack. "I took good care of it. I made my own book cover for it out of a brown paper bag so it would stay in good condition. We are required to do that here with our text books."

I opened the sack and took the book out. It was in the same condition since the day I gave it to her. I opened the front cover just to check if it was the autographed copy. I returned it to the sack which I placed into my backpack.

"Thanks for letting me use it. Sorry I didn't get to see you before now," she said quietly.

"That's okay," I said, zipping up my backpack. "How was Florida?"

"I didn't go to Florida. Luanne was trying to take us but Betty wouldn't let her. She wasn't allowed to take us out of the state."

"Oh," I said, absorbing her words. "Well, even if you didn't, why didn't you say goodbye when you left Giles? Brad's been heartbroken!" I hoped she felt bad about this bit of information. I was a tad jealous of her being on his mind all the time, so I couldn't resist throwing it in there.

"Michelle, it's a long story." She put her hand to her chest and took a deep breath. Her fiery auburn hair blew in the breeze, dancing around her shoulders. "I am a foster kid and I move around a lot."

"Yeah, but you had my phone number!"

Her eyes searched the schoolyard again. "I don't wanna waste time talking about why I didn't say goodbye."

"Then what do you wanna talk about? Maybe Sean Watson getting killed?"

She started breathing heavy, like she was afraid. "I heard about that. Look, I can't really say much. My foster father is watching me all the time. I can't have a phone and I can't drive."

"You gotta be kidding me!" I said. "He is that strict?"

She nodded. "I gotta get away from him."

"What happened? Is he abusing you?" I asked, grabbing her shoulders. "What's going on?"

She shook her head. "It's not like abuse. Him and his friends creep me out. He is constantly with me. The only time I'm without him is here at school. I also think he comes into my room at night to make sure I'm asleep."

"Well, Luanne was strict on you too," I said, taking a step back from her. "You couldn't have friends over or have your own cell phone with her either. What's with all the secrets? What happened to that guy that was buried in the backyard? Did you know him?" I threw out as many questions as I could since it felt like our time was limited.

"The police asked me all about that," she said. "The guy was from Luanne's past. That's why she was so strict. She was always looking over her shoulder, thinking someone was after her. I overheard her on the phone. Someone called and she told them there was no Luanne who lived there. Whoever it was kept calling. It was like her past caught up with her."

"Who is the guy? The police still don't know, so do you? What's the deal with her past?"

"The only thing I know about her past is that she was orphaned too."

I had a feeling she was lying to me. She couldn't look me straight in the eye when I asked the questions.

"Was she having an affair with a married man?" I asked.

She looked back at me and straightened her shoulders, her eyes narrowing. "No. Who said that?"

"Everyone."

She shook her head. "Sean was trying desperately to get with her. She blew him off, then he got upset and ran to Betty Fitzgerald from Guardian Angels Family Services. She contacted Mom to tell her we were to be taken away."

"Mom?" I asked, confused.

"Luanne," she said, "Luanne was the next best thing to

a real mother." She stopped for a few seconds and looked around the schoolyard once more. She pinched her lips together, on the verge of crying. "I gave the officer the post-card she sent me from Florida." She let out a sob and buried her face in her hands.

I put my arms around her. "What postcard?" I had no idea she was this messed up.

"It was her suicide note," she said, wiping her eyes with her sleeve. Her hands were trembling as she talked between sobs. "I had my mail forwarded after moving in with Mr. Becker."

Her voice was so shaky, I thought she was going to have a meltdown right there. I had no idea how to handle this as I kept trying to comfort her the best I could.

"That's his name?"

She nodded. "Michelle, she said she was continuing on her journey into the Atlantic and she had no place left to go."

My mouth dropped. I didn't expect news of Luanne committing suicide. "That's what she wrote on the post-card? Did you tell the police?"

She nodded again. "They are searching for her car, but I don't know if they will ever find it. It sounds like she drove it into the ocean." She seemed to be straightening up, try-ing to keep it together as she explained.

"Who was the guy buried in the yard?" I asked, letting go of her.

"His name was Carl. Look, I'm not one hundred percent sure it's him, but that's the guy who was after her. I heard her on the phone once ask who the caller was, and then she said that name like she was questioning it. She was petrified after that, always pacing the floor, losing sleep."

"Did you tell the police this? Why don't they know who he is?"

"Mr. Becker was with me at the police station."

"Yeah, I saw you leave. That's when I followed you home."

"Well, I can't tell them about this Carl guy when he is there with me."

"Why not?" I was confused as ever, but hoped to get the truth out of her. It dawned on me if anyone was looking for her inside the school.

"Becker is connected with this guy. I overheard him talking one night when I was supposed to be asleep. Carl's family helped him get that house and his finances in order. Now he is paying them back. Betty Fitzgerald took a bribe from him so he could have me."

I wondered if Brad found that part out. My guess was no, or he would have told me. I remembered him mentioning something about paying big bucks for a child.

"Where is Deedee?" I asked.

"She was fostered by someone else just after we went back to Betty. She was lucky. They are keeping me to see if I know where Luanne is. They want her dead."

"But she *is* dead." I tried not to blurt it out, but this whole story sounded far fetched.

She shook her head. "Not necessarily," she whispered.

I couldn't grasp what she was trying to tell me. I was getting frustrated. "What are you talking about? You gotta go to the police and tell them this! Whatever it is you know! At least about Betty taking bribes like that! This is unbelievable!" I put my hands up to my forehead, trying to grasp everything.

"I have called the police before when a foster parent has abused me. Nothing is ever done about it." She was still whispering and looking around like she was paranoid. She looked back at me with red rimmed eyes. "Becker will kill me. I can't take down an organized crime family."

"WHAT?" I blurted out, extending my hands.

Organized crime? I thought. Was that like the mafia? Suddenly, all the rumors came rushing back to me. That had to have been made up by someone unless Luanne's past got out somehow. Nobody went into detail about the mafia, just that they killed Katie's family.

"Shhhhhh, keep your voice down! I don't wanna-"

In a blink of an eye, a vehicle pulled up. Everything happened so fast, I didn't know what hit me as I was grabbed by the neck and thrown in.

Chapter 33

"Katie!" I tried to yell over a hand that was over my mouth. I bit down and tasted dry salty skin.

"OOOWWW!" A man howled in pain. "You little bitch!"

A slap came next, right to the side of my face. I fell down onto the seat, feeling the sting rise up to my eye.

"Leave her alone!" another man demanded from the front seat.

I looked up and noticed his sandy colored hair. It had to be Mr. Becker. The man who hit me was a muscular bald freaky looking guy. He wore sunglasses that had perfectly rounded frames which were too small for his face. He appeared to have no neck since his double chin shot straight down to his collar bone. He wore all black and reminded me of a biker. I found it strange that he had on a leather jacket in this nice weather.

It took me a minute to realize my backpack was still on. I didn't dare mess with it in case one of them took it from me. I looked around and noticed that I was in a van.

Probably the same one I followed. I tried to open the window, but the crank wouldn't turn.

"Don't even think about that, little lady!" the bald man said. He pulled out a knife and pointed it at me.

I started breathing hard. I sat against the door and put my feet up on the seat. I drew my knees up and wrapped my arms around my legs.

What was going to happen now? I thought as I quietly started sobbing. Where were we going? To Brookview Estates? Would Katie call the police from the school? Was she going to help me? Then it crossed my mind that maybe she set this up. Maybe she knew this was going to happen. She was looking around quite a bit when I was talking to her. She knew, I thought. She betrayed me.

"We're takin' a trip," the bald man said. "In case you are wonderin', we need to question you."

"About what?" I asked quietly, my voice almost a whisper.

"Oh, I think you know what." He started trimming his fingernails with the knife.

I shook my head. "No, I don't."

I really didn't know, but thought it had something to do with the dead body. I also thought these two were the ones who killed Sean.

"Stop talking!" Mr. Becker said, looking into his rearview mirror. "We will find out what she has going on up there in that pretty little skull of hers soon enough."

My heart pounded like a drum. I looked down and I

could actually see my shirt moving up and down with each heartbeat. I'm gonna die, I thought. The only thing I could do was fight. If I could get a hold of Baldy's knife somehow, I'd start swinging and never stop. I'd have to make a sudden move, but he seemed to be too quick with the way he was watching me. I couldn't fight this guy. He was way too strong. Just as this thought occurred to me, he put his knife away and took a thin black scarf from his jacket pocket. I told myself not to panic. I focused on his sunglasses.

"We didn't have time to do this when we grabbed you," Baldy said.

Oh no, he was going to tie me up, I thought. I can't be confined. I will go crazy. The closet incident came back to me. I did my best not to panic as my mind raced, trying to think of how to get out of this. There was no way I could go back into another enclosed space. I would rather them kill me quick and get it over with, I thought.

He then stretched out the scarf and grabbed my neck. I did what came to mind. I kicked my legs as hard as I could, hitting him in the groin.

"OOOOOOOWWWWW!" He howled even more. "STOP THE VAN!" he uttered through clenched teeth, holding his private area. He still had the knife in his hand.

"You know I can't do that!" Becker said angrily. "Can't you restrain a teenage girl? Maybe I need to call the boss and see if I can get a better business associate."

"LIKE HELL!" he yelled.

He then grabbed a fistful of my hair and yanked it. I

screamed as he pulled my head down to the seat. He positioned his leg across my neck to hold my head still. I thought he was going to choke me. Just then, the scarf blinded me. I was in darkness and I felt panic coming. My breathing increased even more and I started to cry. I hated myself for weakening.

"You should have behaved yourself and we wouldn't have to do this the hard way!" he said, still grunting while holding onto my hair.

The ride didn't last much longer. The van stopped before the driver's door opened and shut. Baldy continued to pull me by my hair until I was out of the car. I cried the whole time.

"You want me to gag you?" he said harshly. "Shut up!"

I stopped crying out loud while he held on to my shoulder and walked me. Mr. Becker must have been the one to grab my other shoulder. Baldy was almost yanking my arm out of the socket. The material in the scarf was so thin, sunlight was coming through. I barely made out an outline of what appeared to be a white house, if it was a house we were going into. We stopped and I heard a door open. It was a high pitched whiny sound like a screen door would make. They led me quite a ways inside, then I heard a creaking sound. Another door was opening.

"Now take it one step at a time," Mr. Becker said nicely. "We got you."

They were leading me to a basement. A sob escaped my throat when I smelt the musty damp air.

"Knock that cryin' shit off!" Baldy demanded. "I'm get-tin' sick of hearin' it."

When we finally got to the bottom, they sat me down. A weight was lifted off my shoulders from the backpack being taken. They took my arms and put them behind me, tying something around my wrists. My body was trembling. I couldn't do anything. I did my best to move my hands around, but I was stuck. Whatever they used to tie my wrists with, was burning my skin.

They moved to my ankles but I started kicking. I must have gotten Baldy in the face. My foot hit something and I heard clanking on the concrete floor. I thought I knocked his sunglasses off.

"Hey!" He yelled. I felt him grab my neck. "Stop the kicking!"

His breath was horrific, reminding me of beer and hot dogs. I spat, trying to aim for his face. I wasn't sure if I got him.

He started to choke me as I gasped for air. That made me kick even more.

"Hey!" Becker yelled. "Don't kill her! Help me with her ankles!"

"I will let you go," he told me, "but if you try that shit again, I will cut your throat! I don't care what he says! No little girl can beat me, you got it?"

I stopped kicking. I just wanted to breathe. He let go and I gasped, breathing in as much air as I could. My mind raced. I didn't know what they had in store. I was waiting for a gun shot to the head, if they even had a gun. I didn't remember seeing one.

"Okay, now we are going to take off your blindfold," Mr. Becker said. "Are you ready?"

"Yes," I answered in a shaky voice.

I so wanted to say his name but I wasn't sure if Katie was supposed to tell me. If I knew for sure that she betrayed me, I would have. If she didn't, would she have called the police? She saw the whole thing. Nobody was with me to help. How was I going to get out of this? I felt panic come on again as I breathed rapidly, trying to catch my breath. I felt as if I were suffocating in this basement.

"Okay," Mr. Becker said, after taking off my blindfold and sitting across from me. "Stop breathing so hard or you will pass out."

"I can't," I said between breaths. I looked around as my eyes rested on the cob webs in the corners of the walls and ceiling. Green mold appeared to be seeping through the walls made of cement blocks. I was repulsed as goose bumps formed all over my body. "Where am I?" I asked, shivering.

"Somewhere not pretty," he said. "Look we just want to know where Luanne White is. Since that's her name now."

Baldy was standing tall next to his chair, his arms folded. His sunglasses remained on his face.

I never even knew Luanne, just from what Katie told me. "I don't know," I told him. "I haven't seen her since she went to Florida."

"Florida?" Mr. Becker asked. "Why did she go there?"

I shrugged. "I guess for a vacation during Spring Break."

"Hmmm," he said. "Something tells me you know more than just that."

I shook my head. "No! I don't!" I was getting agitated sitting there. I didn't care if my wrists were burning. I continued to wiggle around. I could live with burn marks and cuts.

"Sit still!" Baldy yelled.

"We waited long enough for Katie to tell you something. And she had to say *something*."

"No!" I said louder.

"You think we're stupid?" Baldy said.

"Get her backpack," said Mr. Becker.

Baldy took it from the floor and unzipped the front pocket. He pulled out my cell phone. "Well, you won't be needing this," he said, throwing it down on the ground and crushing it with a stomp of his black boot.

My life flashed before my eyes. I yelled as loud as I could. My throat was dry, almost burning. Baldy appeared in front of me and slapped me in the same place he did before. The sting was a lot worse.

"Now!" Baldy demanded. "I told you to stop that or I will gag you!"

Well, then I couldn't answer your questions, I thought.

"Whiny little girls!" he added, returning to my backpack. He took out my school books and the one book that started this whole thing.

"Hmmm," he said. "You must be one smart cookie. Accounting student."

I nodded.

"Good with numbers?" he asked.

"I guess," I answered, confused over his question. "I had trouble with that class."

"What did Katie tell you?" Mr. Becker asked, getting back to the matter at hand.

"She just thanked me for my book I let her borrow. She needed it for a history paper."

"There isn't a history book in here," Baldy said. "You just come up with that one?"

"No," Mr. Becker said. "She is actually right. Katie told me she had this book that needed to be returned. I thought she meant to her old school."

"So, you had a history book from school all to yourself?" Baldy asked.

I shook my head. "It's mine. Just easier to read than text books are. The teacher let her use it for reference."

"This ugly brown one?" he asked, thumbing through it.

I found it ironic that he was calling a book ugly when he looked ten times worse.

"Katie always had her nose in a book," Mr. Becker said.

I kept quiet. Katie and I both loved to read but she was more book smart than I was. I had a feeling he knew this.

"Hmmm, sounds like a love story," Baldy said, throwing

it down on the floor with the rest of my books.

A puff of dust flew up with every book drop. He looked through my spiral notebook but didn't see anything of interest so he threw that down too. It landed open, face down. "Well, we have nothin' Bob," he said to Mr. Becker.

"What does this have to do with Luanne?" I asked, getting back to the reason I was tied up in this creepy basement.

"The book?" he asked. "Nothing. There is a contract out on her and we have to find her."

I acted ignorant as I looked at them dumbstruck. I did my best to lie. This was life or death so I thought of something I didn't know the facts about, like where I was. "Contract? Did she quit a job or something?" Maybe they were supposed to kill her or take her to someone. I wasn't sure which. Where was I? Who's house is this? I kept these thoughts going as they talked to me.

They laughed. "Job?" Mr. Becker asked. "She doesn't know anything," he told Baldy.

"Well, we can't let her go!" Baldy said.

The panic started coming again. What were they going to do with me? I thought. Kill me? Dump me in a hole like that Carl guy? Put me in a small enclosed space for me to rot?

"Let me try again," Mr. Becker said. "Does the name Carl Fabrizzi mean anything to you?"

Baldy looked at him wide-eyed. I had a feeling he wasn't supposed to say Carl's name.

I shook my head, hoping to appear dumb. The last name threw me since I never heard Katie say it.

"She doesn't know," Mr. Becker said again.

Just then there was a knock coming from upstairs.

"What the hell?" Baldy said.

"Go answer it," Mr. Becker instructed.

Baldy exhaled like he was being inconvenienced as he climbed the stairs. I heard his footsteps walk across above me. His steps made me able to make out where the front door was. Mr. Becker had his eyes on the ceiling the whole time. I heard muffled voices for a few minutes and then a scuffle. A loud thud hit the floor above us.

Mr. Becker jumped up from his chair. "Don't make a sound." He said quietly.

I didn't obey him. This was it. It was now or never. I needed help so I screamed as loud as I possibly could. It was a blood curdling shriek that filled the basement.

He grabbed me by my neck and started choking me. He was gripping my neck so tight, much tighter than Baldy did. I thought I was going to die. I couldn't breathe. I saw myself dead on this filthy basement floor.

Were they coming downstairs to get me? I thought as he shook me.

I looked into his light blue eyes. They weren't beautiful like most baby blues were. They were evil. He wasn't the nice guy he tried to make me believe. He was a monster. His face was beet red as he grunted, trying his best to squeeze the life out of me. Just then a shadow came over me and

Becker let go. He tumbled onto the floor as I coughed and gagged. I was stuck in the chair, so I couldn't even cover my mouth. Coughing, I sucked in the musty basement air which made me gag even more.

Then I felt someone untying me.

"Are you okay?" a familiar voice asked.

I nodded, coughing with my head down. I felt hands on my shoulders as I was being brought out of the chair. I stood and looked up. I saw the most beautiful creature in front of me. It was Brad. Brad? I thought. Did I die? I didn't know what happened next as dizziness came over me and then everything went black.

The next thing I knew, I was moving. I was on my back and my arms wouldn't move. Was I tied up again? My eyes snapped open, but I wasn't aware of my surroundings. I tried to scream, but my voice went in and out. I couldn't get a loud scream to come out of my throat. I panicked and fidgeted wildly.

"Michelle, stop it!" I heard someone say. "You are fine!"

I looked toward the voice and saw Brad looking down at me. He had me by my right hand.

"We're going to take you up the stairs," another voice said.

I was on a stretcher, gasping for air, trying to calm down, but I couldn't seem to get calm.

"It's okay," Brad said again.

I was being carried. As I went through a doorway, I

felt the stretcher land on a surface. I was being wheeled through a kitchen area, then a living room. I spotted Katie by another door. A door where daylight shined through. Wonderful daylight!

"Katie!" I uttered as loud as I could. I reached out but I kept moving past her. She gave me a smile. I thought I saw tears in her eyes.

Relief swept over me as I was released into the sunshine. I closed my eyes. Sobs escaped me and I could not stop crying. The most nightmarish incident of my life just came to an end.

They hooked me up to an IV in the ambulance. Sirens rang loudly in my ears. Brad stayed with me the whole time, holding my hand, consoling me as I cried the whole way to the hospital.

Chapter 34

I calmed down when the nurses were talking to me while I was being admitted.

"You've been through a terrible ordeal, hon," one older nurse said to me. "Just take it easy."

I was checked out and held for observation overnight. Nothing was wrong with me physically. I felt sore around my neck. I had a throbbing headache, hoping the medicine in my IV would take it away. I also had burn marks on my wrists from the rope they used to tie me up with.

Shortly after this, Mom and Dad showed up. Mother look strung out like she had been up for hours. Her hair was a mess, sticking out all over and she was pale faced.

"You okay, Sweetie?" Dad asked, taking my hand.

Mom couldn't say anything. All she did was cry.

"I'm sorry, Mom," I whispered.

She hugged me and didn't let go for a long time. "I'm just glad you're okay," she said between sobs.

"When you are more relaxed and can see things clearer, the officer would like to talk to you again," Dad told me.

"He may have to come up here to talk to you since they want to know what happened right away."

"Did they get them?" I asked. "Tell me they got the bastards!"

Mom's eyes bulged as she looked over at my dad. I was sure she was surprised at my choice of words.

"Yes," he said, nodding, holding out a cup of water. "They got the bastards."

I took a drink as the ice cold soothed my throat. "I will tell them everything, I remember what happened. I wanna tell them!" My hands were shaking as I held the cup.

Tears ran down my mom's face. She reached over and stroked my hair. "Just calm down, Sweetheart," she said. "I'm so sorry."

"What are you sorry about?" I asked her before taking another drink.

"I just think you wouldn't have been so adamant on cutting school to find out the truth if I would have just helped you with this. I'm so sorry."

Just then my backpack occurred to me. "Where are my books?" I asked, looking at Brad. "Did they get them out of there?"

He nodded. "They were picking them up as we got you on the stretcher." He walked over to the closet and opened the door. "They're in here," He said, holding up my backpack.

I was relieved, but then it dawned on me about how I was found. Everything happened so fast. "Wait, how did you know where I was? Who called the police?"

"I saw you leave the school," Brad said, walking toward my bed. "You were holding your stomach when you went to the office and I was wondering what was wrong. You looked really tired this morning when I talked to you. I just watched you walk out of the building so I went out the back to my car. That's when I saw you going toward the bus stop. Then I knew something was up."

"Why didn't you yell or something?"

"Would you have told me where you were going?" he asked.

I shook my head reluctantly. "No, I guess not."

"I had a feeling you knew more than you were telling me. You just seemed preoccupied the last couple of times we talked."

"Sorry I kept this from you. I didn't know how you would react."

"I know," he said. "I just don't get why Katie didn't call the police before now."

"She was scared," I told him. "She was freaking out when we were talking by the school." I explained to him that she had called the police before with other foster parents and she was never without Mr. Becker unless she was in school. I also told him about the postcard Luanne sent her.

We all sat in silence for a moment. I remembered Katie saying that Luanne wasn't necessarily dead, whatever that meant, but I didn't bring it up.

"Brad," Mom said, breaking the silence. "If it wasn't for

you, who knows what would have happened."

"Well, Katie called the police too," he said.

So, she didn't betray me, I thought, feeling much better about her.

"Yes, but you followed her to the house," Mom said. "Katie wasn't sure where she was."

"You did?" I asked him.

"Yeah, I called the police when I saw that van pull up. I didn't actually see them take you since the van was in my way. I parked further down a side street so I was catty corner from the school."

"Well, you must know," Mom continued, looking at Brad, "Michelle likes you very much."

"Mom!" I gasped. It hurt my neck when I turned to her.

"Michelle, you know it's true. She likes you Brad," she told him. "It was horrible how you misled her. She was so excited that night you took her out."

He looked down. "Sorry," he said. "I was stupid. I was holding onto something that wasn't going to happen."

It was ironic that I thought the same thing about us. "Where is Katie?" I asked.

"At the police station," he answered. "They have a lot of questions for her."

"Mom, since we are being truthful," I began, "there is a reason I wanted to find Katie to begin with."

She looked serious, her eyebrows plunging down between her eyes. "What is it?"

"Brad could you take my books out of my bag?" I asked him.

He grabbed all of them, including the novel my grandmother left me.

I held out my hand. "Can you hand me the small brown one?"

He handed it over and I opened it.

Mom noticed the autograph on the first page. "That's the book Grandma gave you! What's it doing here?"

I swallowed painfully before going on. Dad handed me the cup of water again. I took a drink which eased the pain. "I let Katie borrow it. It was for a paper on The Great Depression."

"She couldn't find a history book about it?"

"This was easier to read and more entertaining. You know history books are boring," I said matter-of-factly.

She took a deep breath. "Okay, I understand." She seemed to be struggling with understanding that I loaned out the book.

"I'm sorry, but Katie got me through accounting at the worst times. I was afraid I was going to have to drop it and I love Ms. Runyon."

"What about Tami?" she asked. "Brad's in the class too."

"Yes, but Katie was the smartest."

"She helped us all," Brad interjected.

"Anyway, I just wanted to tell you about this," I said.

"What happened to the cover?" Mom asked, pointing to the brown paper.

"Katie made this to protect it." I tried my best, prying off the scotch tape on the edge of the paper. I had to tear it a little to take it off. I looked at the original cover trimmed in gold. Grandma's memory came back briefly. Then I noticed something about the brown paper.

"What's wrong," Brad asked. "You look puzzled."

I eyed the inside of the brown paper. It was Katie's handwriting. "Oh my God!" I said louder than my throat would allow.

Everyone came over to the bed and looked down at the paper. We all read it quietly to ourselves.

It read: ROBERT BECKER IS FOSTERING ME IN BROOKVIEW ESTATES. I OVERHEARD HIM TALKING TO SOME GUY WHO STOPPED BY WHEN THEY THOUGHT I WAS ASLEEP. THEY SAY LUANNE KILLED A MAN NAMED CARL FABRIZZI. IT SOUNDS LIKE SHE CHANGED HER NAME AND LEFT HIM. SHE LEARNED A LOT FROM HIM ABOUT COVERING UP AND LEAVING NO TRACES, BUT HE FOUND HER. BETTY FITZGERALD TOOK US AWAY FROM HER. CHECK HER OUT. GUARDIAN ANGELS CHILD SERVICES. SHE TAKES BRIBES. LUANNE LEFT FOR FLORIDA AND ENDED UP KILLING HERSELF. SHE ALWAYS TOLD ME SHE WANTED TO GIVE ME A GOOD LIFE. TO ME, SHE WAS A REAL MOTHER, BUT DEEDEE RESENTS HER. SHE THINKS LUANNE TOOK OFF WITHOUT US AFTER PROMISING US

A FLORIDA VACATION. IF YOU EVER SEE HER, COULD YOU TELL HER THE TRUTH? I BELIEVE THAT LUANNE FOUGHT CARL IN SELF DEFENSE. SHE WAS SCARED, STAYING AWAKE ALL NIGHT SOMETIMES. I HEARD HER CRYING, BUT SHE WOULD NEVER TELL ME WHY. IF YOU FIND THIS, TAKE THIS TO THE AUTHORITIES. BECKER IS WATCHING ME ALL THE TIME. I'M SCARED OF HIM.

Staring at the paper, we were speechless.

"I hope she tells the police this," I said.

"If not, give them this," Mother said. "She wanted you to find this."

"She was smart, wasn't she?" I said.

"Yeah, she called the police at the same time I did. They told me a call came in on another line with the same incident," Brad explained.

"And you knew was it her?" Mom asked him.

He nodded. "I asked her when she showed up at the house with the police."

I folded the paper and put in inside the book.

"I am so glad I followed you," Brad said, taking my hand. Looking at me with his sweet blue eyes, it was at that moment when I found out that I loved him. I knew it with all my heart.

Chapter 35

Brad left after visiting hours were over, but my parents were allowed to stay. Tami tried stopping in, but the nurses ran her out saying family only were allowed to stay indefinitely.

I had just finished half of a ham and cheese sandwich with chocolate pudding before Officer Avalos arrived. He was allowed to see me later since it was the best time for no interruptions. Mom and Dad agreed to step out of the room so I could tell my story. I was glad because I didn't want to be intimidated with Mom listening in.

"You are one lucky girl," he told me.

I nodded, "I know."

"You doing okay?"

I shrugged. "I'm afraid to go to sleep."

"Nightmares?"

I nodded again.

"The house you were held in belonged to Ramon Johnston."

"Who's that?"

"The guy who took you."

"Baldy?" I asked.

He chuckled. "Yeah, you could say that. Now just take your time," he said, taking out his notepad, "and tell me what happened to you."

I went slowly through the whole story. From when I followed Katie home from the police station to when I passed out. I was breathing rapidly when I finished.

"Here," he said, giving me the cup of water. "It's okay now. The guys are put away."

My hand trembled as I handed him the brown paper Katie wrote on.

He unfolded it and read it. He didn't look surprised to read the words. He probably already knew since Katie talked to him. "Thanks. Can I keep this?"

"Yes," I uttered, slowing my breathing. I started to cry again. The cries turned into loud sobs.

Officer Avalos put his arm around me and I heard the door open.

"What's going on?" I heard Mom ask.

"She just went through everything as it happened," he told her. "It's okay. I've seen this happen many times."

"I'm so scared," I said between sobs. I wanted Brad there with me. I wanted to see his face so I could be calm again. I wanted to forget this.

"Honey, they are taken care of," Mom said.

I shook my head. "This guy had connections!" They looked at me as if I were telling a fictional story. "Katie said it was organized crime." The words WITNESS RELOCATION flashed before my eyes.

"WHAT?" Mom blurted out.

"Well, Katie helped us with that," the officer said.

"How?" Mom asked.

"We know who was involved."

Looking at my parents, I took a deep breath. Relief swept over me at that moment. "Is she gonna be okay?"

He nodded. "Yes, but you may not see her again."

Dad nodded and I understood, but Mom still looked puzzled.

"What do you mean?" she asked him.

"I can't discuss it anymore," he told them.

"I will explain it to you," Dad told her.

I was a little sad that Katie would be relocating. She was used to moving around, but I was really missing her at that moment.

I healed after a week upon returning from the hospital. Tami stayed with me almost every evening, until it was time to go home. She brought me my homework and slept over every weekend.

The trial took place three months later, in a big city a few hours away from Giles. Brad, Tami, and I weren't allowed to go to the trial since we were on the witness list, but we stood outside to hear the verdict.

After the guilty verdict was announced and the wonderful feeling of relief swept over us, our parents wanted to get a bite to eat at a steakhouse nearby. Instead of joining them, the three of us went to The Big Scoop across the street.

It was chilly when we walked in. I rubbed my hands vigorously up and down my arms as we ordered at the counter. Everything was colored in red and white down to the napkin holders. Stools were at the counter where people could sit, but we decided on a booth.

Shortly after we sat down, Tami's brother Brian walked in and spotted us.

"Hey!" He waved to us from the counter.

Many people were staring. I gathered it was his face piercings and gelled out hair that brought on the attention. This surprised me since we were in a big city and many freaky people roamed the streets.

After taking his vanilla ice cream cone from the server, he slid in to the booth across from me.

"That was some trial," he said. "Old Man Nichols cracks me up."

"Oh, what did he have to say?" Tami asked, sucking down her root beer float.

"Never mind that, what happened?" I asked him, scooping up a spoonful of my hot fudge sundae.

"First of all, that Fabrizzi family ain't nothin'."

"What do you mean?" I asked.

"Well, they're not as big as you would think for a freakin' crime family."

"That's good," said Brad.

"Yeah, but they have a lot of connections," I pointed out. "How else would they have found Luanne?"

"That was because of that stupid landlord," Brian explained, twirling his cone around while licking the ice cream. It made me wonder if his tongue piercing got in the way.

"Yeah, he was a prick all right!" Brad said in a hostile tone.

"They found him first. He gave them information on where she was, but demanded money first."

"That sounds like him," Brad said. Then he looked at Tami when he added, "I knew he was a slime ball."

Tami stayed silent, but I sensed she wanted to lay into Brad for aiming that statement at her.

"Well," Brian continued, "he did the same thing when Carl's dad sent Bob Becker after him. He claimed to know where Carl was and wanted money for it. Then he kept upping the ante. Now, how stupid is that? He didn't even know this Carl dude."

"Sean's house seemed nice," Tami pointed out. "I only saw the outside, but I thought they already had money." She grabbed her straw with her mouth.

"His old lady did," said Brian. "Well, her family did. They controlled everything. It seems that Sean couldn't leave her and still keep her money, but she could walk out on him. Pretty cool agreement if ya ask me." He then chomped into his cone like he was attacking it. After swallowing, he said, "That bald freaky guy ran over him."

"Oh, so it was Ramon?" I asked.

"Yeah, that Becker dude got his sentence reduced since he ratted him out. He was just a regular guy who needed financial assistance and another crime boss helped him out. This boss dude knew the Fabrizzi's."

"Oh, so they aren't very big, but they have other families they are connected to?" I asked, worried.

"Didn't they give you the option to be relocated like Katie was?" Tami asked me.

I nodded, sitting back from the table contemplating what Brian said. "Yeah, but I didn't want it. My whole family would have to relocate and I couldn't ask them to leave their jobs and our home. I will miss you guys too. There's no way I would want that." I sat back up to the table, picking up my spoon. I eyed the hot fudge slowly dripping from it.

"They will go after Becker before you anyway," said Brian. "He ratted them out. That's how the whole family got put away. That other family, whoever it was, wasn't named off anyway."

Then it dawned on me. "I wonder if that was Becker with him when you were outside the house, spying on him," I told Tami.

She shrugged.

"You said he had blonde hair, right?"

"I guess," she said. "I just peeked through the window once."

We sat there in silence for a few seconds.

"Who gives a shit? He's dead now. You don't mess with a big boss man," Brian said.

While wiping his hands with a napkin, Brian continued. "And that Betty bitch got hers! Twenty-five years for taking bribes and endangering the lives of kids. Serves her fat ass right!"

The people at the next table were looking over at us. Brian wasn't one to lower his voice no matter where he was.

"Oh, and they explained what Luanne did with this Carl dude. They speculated anyway. I guess she hit him over the head with a ball bat or something like that and then when he was laying face down in the kitchen, she yanked him by the hair, pulled his head up and sliced his neck with a knife!" He stuck out his forefinger and drew it across his neck.

"You wanna keep it down over there?" The guy sitting behind him said.

"Sorry, Sir," Brian said without turning to face him. "Anyway, this guy took care of her since she was a teenager. Her parents went to some convenient store, sent her in for something, then took off, abandoning her. I dunno where her sister was. He found her, took her in and ran her life. Sounded like she was in a prison life with him or something. Who knows what all he did with her."

We all looked at each other, but we thought Brian was just speculating. Nothing was known for sure about her private life with Carl.

We'd already heard that just before the trial, Luanne's car was found in the Atlantic. The investigation led them to the area where she had driven off a cliff. They had a witness who saw it happen. It was Luanne's real sister. She went to Florida to find her. The sister claimed to not know Luanne's name since her original name was Sandra Quinn. Rumors were going around that her sister was hiding her somewhere, but everything checked out and Luanne was presumed dead. No body was found.

"Just glad the whole thing is over," Brian said, standing up. "Well, kids, I'm outta here. See ya!" He turned and walked out.

As he got to the door, I noticed two U.S. Marshalls walking in with a girl. She had dark brown hair that was cut short in a pixie style. As she got closer, I noticed her freckles.

I dropped my spoon, jumped up, and hugged her. "Katie! Oh my God!"

She had a big smile on her face as she sat down where Brian had been.

"I had to convince them to let me come in. I saw you guys walk in from across the street."

The U.S. Marshalls were waiting by the counter.

"Where are you going?" I asked her.

"I dunno yet. Some place other than where I've been. I just wanted to apologize."

We all sat there, looking at each other in silence. Tami sat with her arms folded, glaring at Katie. I didn't want her to say anything in the state she seemed to be in. We had been through a lot since Katie left Giles, but I didn't hold it against her.

"Katie," I finally spoke up, "you didn't mean for this to happen."

"No, but I should have called the police right away," she said. "I should have sent your book back when I got taken away, but I wasn't sure if you would really get it with the mail system the way it is."

Tami's eyes narrowed after that post office remark.

I shook my head. "You didn't know it would come to this. I mean, who would have thought they were watching you while you were at the school? You made a smart move, writing all that down inside the book cover."

She nodded. "I was afraid someone would see that, but I put it together tightly to where it wouldn't fall off."

"Well, it was a smart move," Brad said.

"I didn't even know right away who Becker really was," she said. "You went through all of this because of me." She looked over at Brad. "And I'm sorry I didn't say goodbye."

"It's okay," Brad said. He left it at that without taking her hand or putting his arm around her.

Katie looked back at me. "I'm going to find her," she whispered. "I am going to travel when I turn eighteen. I won't stop looking."

I nodded reluctantly. I couldn't see a successful result coming out of this. I just couldn't imagine Katie being able to find her, unless Luanne had dropped her a hint somehow.

"She wanted to live," she whispered, tears forming in her eyes. "She was a great mother."

"Man, the talk of the town was wrong," I said. "You know all the crap we heard?"

"It usually is wrong," said Brad.

Tami loosened up and went back to her root beer float.

"Good luck with everything," I told her, noticing the U.S. Marshalls walking over to retrieve her.

"Thanks for everything," she said before they led her out.

I was going to miss Katie. I held back tears until I went to the bathroom. I told Tami and Brad I needed a minute to myself. A minute turned out to be longer than expected as I tried my best to collect myself and return to the table.

"You okay?" Tami asked. "Your eyes are red."

I nodded, wiping my eyes one more time with my hand. "I'm much better."

Tami and Brad led me out of the ice cream shop a minute later. I took in a breath of fresh air and felt rejuvenated. It was time for a new start with old friends.

Epilogue

I started seeing Brad immediately after the trial. After graduating Giles High, we enrolled in community college together. He was interested in becoming a private investigator. I took a crack at accounting, but then changed my major to journalism. We had one more year until graduation and I had never been more positive about my future.

Tami attended the School of Cosmetology in Marian and Mother employed her as an apprentice. She had so much fun learning and working that she never thought of finding her Mr. Right. Her career seemed more important and she met many guys while doing hair.

During my senior year at college, I got home on a chilly October day. I retrieved the mail. Walking up to the house, I noticed a postcard from Minnesota sandwiched in the middle of the bills, magazines and junk mail. It was a nice peaceful snowy scene that actually made me look forward to winter. Turning it over, I stopped dead in my tracks. The hair stood up on the back of my neck. The message was in

Katie's handwriting.

The postcard read: HI MICHELLE. I AM ENJOYING MY LIFE WITH MY MOM.